I0589812

CYNTHIA MELTON

The Hunt

Nightfall, Book Two

Cynthia Melton

For that bit of rebel in all of us.

1

Boom!

I jumped to my feet, sword drawn, whirling to glance in every direction. "What is it?" I blinked the sleep from my eyes.

"Thunder." Fawke grinned. "Relax, no rain yet, but it's coming. We haven't seen sign of anything in days other than those infernal black birds. They make enough racket to wake all of Soriah."

"We've never seen them outside the forest before." I sheathed my sword and headed to the small campfire where Kira brewed the last of our coffee. We needed to spot a drop soon…if there was anyone in the city to drop supplies for. Another day's walk would take us to the city center. I much preferred the outskirts we'd stuck to so far.

"I guess the birds followed us. Maybe the Malignants will eat them instead of us." Kira handed me a dented metal cup. "You know, like they do the rats."

"Not unless those monsters grow wings they

won't get the birds." Dante accepted a cup of his own.

"No breakfast?" Gage frowned.

Kira shook her head. "Supplies are running low. We need to ration."

"Someone will have to go into the city and find scavengers, scouts, hunters, anything," Ezra said. "We've another two days before we reach the first possible site for an arsenal." He stood and grabbed his pack from the wagon.

"No, I'll go." I sighed. "You're the best person to read that map. Find shelter out of the rain." I donned my leather suit, Fawke doing the same. I'd known without asking that he'd accompany me.

"Into the belly of the beast we go." He squared his shoulders.

"It's nothing new." Nor less terrifying. I checked all my weapons, hoping we wouldn't have to use them. Firing the gun would alert anyone around to our location. I preferred to remain anonymous. Right now, Soriah thought us all dead. Just the way I wanted it.

We headed across a field of concrete and dried weeds as the first raindrops fell. Since the rain acted like acid on skin, hence our rubber suits, we didn't worry about Malignants. They stayed inside. We hadn't seen them since leaving Rebel City, but once we entered the city ahead of us, we'd hear and smell them. My blood chilled at the thought.

After an hour of walking, we passed the first toppled building. Gas fires still burned, filling the air with an acrid odor. "I hadn't missed those."

"Me either," Fawke said. "They're good for

nothing but lighting our way and keeping the chill at bay."

"I prefer the trees we left behind." I mourned leaving Rebel City more than I had Soriah, which was strange since my mother still resided in Soriah. How had she taken the news of my death? Someday, I'd see her face again and the joy reflected in her eyes.

We slipped through an opening in an iron fence and into a courtyard. A fountain, empty of water, rose from the center. Skyscrapers, windows long gone, towered over us. From my right came the shriek of a malignant. I shuddered, grateful for the rain.

"What day is it?" I glanced over my shoulder at Fawke.

"Sunday, I think."

"Then, if Soriah sent others, they'll be getting a drop." The question was where? The city sprawled in every direction. We could be close or very far away. At least seeing a chopper would let us know whether we were alone out there. I'd fight for those supplies. We'd never accomplish our mission without food. I hoped whoever might be in the city would know enough to stay away from the center. It was safer on the outskirts and made a supply drop easier.

My stomach growled, and I fished inside my suit for the protein bar inside. I bit into it, the taste of sawdust filling my mouth. It wasn't much, but it would give me energy. Sitting on a low wall, I surveyed the gray sky for signs of a white parachute.

Something moved, but not what I expected. If I hadn't been looking, I'd have missed the slate gray chute floating down. I hadn't heard the chopper over the occasional rumble of thunder. "They changed the color." To make it harder for scouts and thieves?

"Let's go." Fawke led the way at a run.

The drop wasn't close, but we could make it in half an hour if we ran without stopping. We stopped at the edge of a pothole filled parking lot. No Malignants shrieked from nearby buildings, still safely out of the rain. Normally, they waited for a human to venture out for the crate.

Not seeing anyone, we headed across the lot and gripped the handles of the crate. Not as large as we were used to, which led me to believe whatever Stalkers the drop was intended for weren't as large as the seven of us. Still, anything would help.

We carried it under an alcove and used a bar Fawke picked up from the ground to pry open the lid. A bit of coffee, water purification tablets, silver packets of dried meals. It was something.

"That's ours." A voice cracked, then the speaker cleared his throat.

I turned to stare into the faces of three young men around my age. "We got to it first."

"Only because it's raining." The one with black stripes on his face glared, shoving a wool hood away from his face. "Step back, and we won't have to fight you."

I laughed. "That's a fight you'd lose. How many of you are there?"

"Twenty." His gaze flickered toward his comrades.

He lied. The crate would barely feed the three of them.

"Have you seen any scouts?"

"What?" His brow furrowed. "Who are you?"

"Crynn Dayholt. Former Stalker."

"Former? You can't quit this job." He snorted. "You're in it for the long haul or until death claims you."

"Nope." I reached for the handle again. "This is Fawke. Come with us or stay, it doesn't matter to me." I started walking, my shoulders tense, expecting an attack.

"Wait." Footsteps pounded behind us. "Let us join you. We can't fight those things ourselves, and we need what's in that crate. Come back to our camp and let's talk."

I arched a brow at Fawke. "What do you think?"

He shrugged. "Not sure we can trust them, but I don't mind slitting a throat if I have to."

The leader paled. "You can trust us. We have shelter."

I nodded. "Lead the way."

"Awesome. I'm Jay, this is Ryan and Lark. I've been here a month, those two only a matter of a few weeks." He pulled his hood back over his head.

Green behind the ears. I shook my head, remembering my first month of being a Stalker. Hell was the only word to describe what I'd jumped into. Luckily, my group had experienced fighters.

We followed them to the sorriest shelter I'd ever seen. Blankets lay strewn around a gas fire under a fallen building that lay propped on a concrete wall. They could be attacked from at least two directions at any given time. How were they still alive? They were either the luckiest people I knew or the dumbest. Maybe both.

"Why aren't you inside?" I dropped my end of the crate.

"Those things live in the buildings." Jay sat on one of the folded blankets. "We've managed not to have to fight them so far."

"You find a place with only one entrance. Put a dead malignant out front. They can't smell you that way. Not over that stench." I perched on the crate, laying my sword across my knees. "You've not fought once? What do you do all day?"

"Stay here." He leaned on his elbow. "We weren't really given orders other than to kill Malignants. I'd rather not risk my life."

We didn't need inexperienced fighters, but we did need the supplies. I glanced around the makeshift shelter. Three blankets, three swords, two daggers, a canteen… "You didn't take much from the supply room."

He shrugged. "Food mostly. It's gone now."

"You weren't told at all what to expect out here?"

"I had no idea what a malignant was," Dirk said. "I thought maybe it was a rodent. We've seen rats, eaten a few, but those pale fleshed monsters were a surprise."

I glanced at Fawke who frowned. He wasn't any more impressed than I was. These three were lucky to be alive.

"How many is in your group?" Jay asked.

"Seven. We're camped outside the city. No Malignants there. We came in looking for supplies. You haven't seen any other humans?"

"Found evidence, but no sightings." Jay put a pot of water over the fire. "We only leave this place for the drop."

"You don't help newcomers when they arrive?" Fawke sat cross-legged on the ground.

"Why? Nobody helped me. Either they find us or they perish, not that anyone has come in over a week."

"Only criminals and newly eighteen-year-olds will arrive." I exhaled heavily trying to decide if taking them with us would have any advantage.

"Tell them about the noise," Ryan said, purifying the water over the fire.

"What noise?" Fawke's lips pressed together.

"Sounds like trucks," Jay said, "but I haven't seen anything like that since leaving Soriah. Only the military has vehicles of that type. Besides, the city is so crowded with debris, how would they get military vehicles in here?"

Worry creased Fawke's face. He motioned his head for me to join him away from the others. "What if Soriah never bought that we were killed?"

"You think they're out here looking for us?"

"Maybe."

"We aren't that important."

"No, but Rebel City is a real threat. If we located them, joined them, that makes us a threat."

My blood chilled. Would Soriah really start a war? Did they expect these three young men to clear the path of Malignants so others could finish what my group had started? Seemed too far-fetched for me. "It doesn't make sense. Something else is going on."

"But what? We cut out our trackers." He glanced at the scar on his forearm. "No one can know that we found the rebels."

"Unless the choppers spotted them." My mouth dried up. "If they did, the army could be going there. We need to warn them."

"Don't you think Soriah would have dropped a bomb and saved themselves the trouble of sending the army?" He shook his head. "Wanna bet they're looking for the arsenals? Wanna bet more that they knew we'd find the survivors, find out about the arsenals? Since we're supposedly dead, they've come looking for the weapons."

My head hurt from the whiplash of all the possibilities of why Soriah would be here.

The familiar sound of the radio monitor clicking on froze me in place.

2

I turned to stare at the face of Sharon, President Cane's right hand. Shock, then amusement flickered across her face.

"Well, it seems I underestimated you, Miss Dayholt." Sharon's smile didn't reach her eyes. "You aren't the obedient warrior I took you for."

"Hello, Sharon." I might be a warrior, but I wasn't Soriah's warrior. Not anymore.

"I must assume you found the rebels and chose not to let me know. This makes you one of them and a fugitive of the law. Since I see Mr. Newton with you, I must also assume the others are still alive." Her features hardened. "I order you three Stalkers to kill these two criminals."

Jay paled. "But…"

"No buts! That is a direct order. There are forces at work far greater than any of you know. To join her means certain death."

I turned to Jay. "Fight or flight? Your choice, but I guarantee Fawke and I will leave the two of you as malignant food. You cannot win."

"Don't listen to her." Sharon's voice rose. "She's nothing but a girl spouting nonsense. There are three of you."

"Don't underestimate her," Fawke said. "She makes two of each of you." He grinned. "I make three. If I'm doing the math right, that gives us fifteen to three. Remember, none of you have ever fought a battle." He gripped his sword.

"You will regret this." Sharon disconnected.

"Well, gentlemen?" I tilted my head, ready to fight if they chose.

"Guess we're going with you." Jay glanced at his group who nodded.

"Give me your arm." I pulled my knife, cutting the tracker from his arm while Fawke did the other two. "Bandage your wound and pack up. Leave the radio behind. We've quite a hike ahead of us." Battle training would take top priority when we joined the rest of our group. We didn't need any handicaps. Not with Soriah coming after us. And come they would.

The rain stopped. I peeled off my suit and stuffed it into my pack. "Keep an eye out for Malignants. They'll venture out now. The going will be dangerous. I hope you had some training before leaving Soriah."

"Some old lady had me fight a hologram." Jay hitched his pack onto his shoulders. "I did okay, after dying a couple of times."

It was something at least. "Ryan and Lark, carry the crate."

"Ryan's our leader." Lark glowered. "We take our orders from him."

"Not anymore," Fawke said. He glanced at Ryan.

10

"Wipe those stripes off your face. Only one person has that privilege now." He jerked his head toward me.

I didn't know why I still wore the black paint on my face marking me as leader. Somehow, they'd become a shield of sorts. A badge of honor. I now co-led with Fawke, taking the thoughts and opinions of our friends into account when making a decision. Still, it wouldn't hurt these three to look at me as a leader and not go their own way.

"Malignants across the courtyard." Fawke stepped in front of the other three. "If they attack, we form a circle, backs together. Do not break rank."

Three Malignants, noses lifted, sniffed, then shrieked. They knew we were here but hadn't yet spotted us.

One of the three men behind me breathed hard, harsh, in spurts. Fear radiated off him in waves.

I glanced back to see Dirk bent over, hands on his knees. "Don't panic. If you do, you'll die."

"We're all dead already. Sharon will sic the army on us." He took a deep breath and straightened. "Why delay the inevitable?"

"Would you rather die by a bullet or be torn apart by those things?" I arched a brow.

"Point taken." He took a deep breath and straightened.

We moved away from the building and into the open. Being unfamiliar with the buildings in the area, I didn't want to be trapped. The rain had dampened the dry grass, making our steps muffled. I put a finger to my lips to signal the others to be quiet.

Keeping a sharp eye on the monsters, I led the

group at a fast pace through the same opening in the wall Fawke and I had taken earlier. The lot on the other side appeared empty. I studied the area for a means of escape if we were outnumbered and spotted a rickety iron ladder going up one side of a building.

I tapped Fawke's shoulder. "We can see whether the army is here from up there. Maybe."

"Worth a go." He waved the others forward. "Leave the crate behind that pile of debris. We're going up. I'll lead, Crynn will take the rear."

The three followed him so close, I thought they'd climb over Fawke. The noise they made on the old ladder caused me to cringe. The ladder shook under my hands and feet. I glanced down, expecting to see Malignants coming our way. Relief filled me to see nothing under me but concrete.

The top of the building showed the faded markings of a helicopter pad, and a large unit I assumed might once have been air conditioning for the large complex. Nowhere to hide if a chopper did fly over.

Hunched over, we made our way to the waist-high wall circling the roof. Fawke motioned for us to stay down as he peered over. He pulled binoculars, courtesy of Rebel City, from his pack and peered through them.

I couldn't see anything with the naked eye other than Malignants skirting the buildings, staying mostly in the shadows. They seemed to be on a mission, noses to the ground and moving at a high speed away from us.

"They're going somewhere in a hurry." I patted Fawke's arm.

He swung the binoculars in the direction they were headed. "Uh oh. A group of scouts crossing a street about a mile ahead." He handed me the binoculars. "We'd never reach them in time to help."

"There's at least ten of them. They should be able to dispose of the threat." I slowly scanned the horizon. "Or the army will save them." I pointed and handed the eyepiece back.

Ryan and his friends were right. They had heard army trucks. Four jeeps, armed with heavy artillery drove slowly just outside the city. Any gunfire would alert them to humans. If...the scouts had a gun. Most used swords or knives.

"It'll be a bloodbath," Dirk said hoarsely. "What if we alert the army to the scout's danger?"

"We'll let them know our location." Fawke looked at him as if a third eye had appeared in the man's forehead. "Are you dense?"

Jay smacked Dirk upside the head. "Weren't you listening to Sharon? We're criminals now."

His face fell. "My father is going to be so disappointed."

I rolled my eyes and tried to come up with a plan and failed miserably. There was nothing we could do without exposing ourselves. "Any sign of where the jeeps are going? It might let us know of a possible location for the arsenal or where their camp is."

"Not that I can see." Fawke shook his head. "We need to get back to our group. There's no way those jeeps can sneak up on them, but I feel too exposed out here."

I agreed and led the way back down the ladder, Fawke taking the rear this time. Dirk and Ryan grabbed the crate and we set off to rejoin our group, counting on the Malignants attention on the scouts to keep us out of immediate danger.

We stopped a few times to let another small group of monsters race past, their attention on other pursuits. The closer we got to the edge of the city, the faster we moved.

As we approached our group, Ezra met us. "You were gone longer than anticipated. We thought you'd perished. Who are they?"

"Former Stalkers." I explained the radio contact from Sharon. "We are officially criminals and are to be shot on sight. Orders of Sharon." I grinned and dropped my pack. "Did you hear the jeeps?"

His eyes widened. "The military is here?"

"Yep. Most likely looking for the same thing we are. Weapons."

"We're no match for them." Dante's shoulders sagged.

"We need to find their camp and disable them." Fawke accepted a cup of water from Gage. "Right now, a large group of Malignants are hunting a group of scouts. We believe the army is on their way to help. Which means communication between the two. I want that ability."

Moses laughed. "So, you want to disable and steal from the army? You've balls of steel, man."

Shrugging, Fawke sat on the edge of one of the wagons. "We can't beat them without evening the odds. If we had communication, we could send these three to Rebel City. We could get help if we need it without using the flares."

Shooting off the flares would give us away as

effectively as firing a gun into the sky. "We're definitely going to need help. Our battle is not only against monsters now." I shucked off my pack and sat on a folded blanket. "Rest up. These three receive their first training come nightfall."

"I like the idea of this Rebel City," Dirk said. "I'm not cut out for this life."

Most people weren't. I'd thought so myself once. Now battle scarred, I still craved the life we could have had on the mountain. Someday, if the Supreme Being willed, I'd have that life. Maybe with Fawke and children.

I glanced in the direction of Soriah. Although too far away to see, I knew my future didn't lie there. I wanted to free my mother, stop the barbaric way of sending young people to clear the world of monsters, but I could never live there again.

A flock of crows flew overhead darkening the sky even more than usual. Again, I wondered why they'd followed us from the mountain. Their food lay in the forest where dead things were for them to feast on. Here, the Malignants kept the city rid of carcasses. Unless the mountain no longer provided the birds with enough to eat.

"Those things creep me out." Gage sat next to me. Once, she'd disliked me because of my closeness to Fawke. Now, she'd found a new blossoming romance in Rebel City and gave me no more grief. "What do you think our chances of succeeding with Fawke's plan are?"

"Good if we follow his lead."

"What about those three? They seem worthless to me."

"One more reason to send them to the mountain, to be replaced with more experienced fighters." I leaned back on my elbows. "Their skittishness will go away with experience and training."

"They'd never make it to the mountain."

Maybe not. But they'd have a chance if they stayed out of the city. Getting help from Rebel City might be our only chance against the army. We had guns, but not nearly enough weapons or manpower for what was coming. Sharon would hunt us with a vengeance. Neither her or the president would take our rebellion without retaliation.

I sighed. At least my mother would know I still lived. A small consolation.

"Are you okay?" Fawke joined us.

"Wondering what our chances of success against an army are." I grinned. "But then, the army doesn't know you."

"Or you." He chuckled. "We'll have to get in and out without discovery. Take what we need, slash some tires…it'll be risky."

"Everything is."

Gunfire erupted in the distance.

3

I climbed the tallest pile of debris near us and called for the binoculars. After Fawke handed them to me, I studied the terrain, making out men in fatigues behind the guns on the jeeps. They mowed down the Malignants with ease.

Why not send the army in first thing? Why send young people barely old enough to know what they wanted from life? I climbed down.

"This doesn't make sense. The army could have had the city cleared by now." I returned the eyepiece to Fawke and wished for the radio we'd left behind. Not that I expected Sharon to answer my questions, but it wouldn't hurt to ask. The woman, full of power, might not think telling us the truth would hurt. With a heavy sigh, I returned to my blankets.

Fawke joined me. "I think the army was held back for other things. Like disposing of the rebels. To send them into the dead city would alert the rebels to their strength. They'd move. Stalkers are more low key, harder to find out about." He traced in the dirt with a stick, making random designs. "There's no hiding the army's presence now."

"Rebel City needs to be warned." I glanced toward the mountain only two days hike away. Far too close. "Dare we go back? We need fighters." Or we could flee with the others, find a new sanctuary.

"No matter where they run, they'll be hunted. It's up to us to stop the army." He stood. "But, I agree. We need fighters. We'll return to the city, tell Jenkins what we know, then return to deal with the trouble here."

"Alright. Everyone up. We can't risk exposure."

Things were tossed willy-nilly onto the wagons and we set off, stopping for short breaks of an hour here and there to rest. No multiple hours of sleep. We'd get a good night's rest once we reached the mountain. Ignoring protests of exhaustion, I pressed the group on until we reached the safety of the trees two days later. Still, I didn't stop. Not until the ramshackle buildings of Rebel City came into sight.

Jenkins, and his right hand man, Lloyd greeted us. "What happened?" Jenkins asked, his brow furrowed. His expression grew graver as I told him about the army and the large group of scouts.

Fawke continued the discussion by telling the man of his plan. "There's no way the army doesn't know we're here. All we can do is slow them down and beat them to the hidden arsenal. To do that, we need experienced fighters."

"Let's discuss this over a meal. You must be hungry."

"Starved," Dante said. "Supplies ran low a few days ago."

Jenkins nodded. "We'll give you more supplies

and as many fighters as you think you need. Just leave some to protect us. We'll head higher up the mountain so we can't be surprised. A couple of our scouts found an abandoned town, mostly overgrown now. It'll suffice as a place of refuge." He headed toward the main community building.

"The higher you go, the easier it'll be for choppers to spot you," I pointed out.

He laughed, motioning to a group of women sewing branches together. "We've been busy weaving a canopy. We won't be easy to spot." He pushed open the door, ordering Lloyd to take the rest of the group to get something to eat while letting me and Fawke inside. "Food will arrive shortly, then rest. I assume you'll be leaving in the morning?"

"Yes. While we cause havoc with the army, the people here can escape." I sat at a rustic, square wooden table.

Jenkins and Fawke took their seats. The leader folded his hands on the table. "How many fighters do you need?"

"The fifteen I left behind, and any you can spare." I glanced up as a woman entered with a tray of venison and vegetables. My stomach growled in response to the tantalizing aroma.

He nodded. "Your people have been training a few of the young men and women. I can give you five."

I hoped for more, but wouldn't argue. "I'll leave the three we found. If they're trained some, they could help defend the others." I cut into the meat.

"The army seems to have a means of communicating with their scouts. I need a runner.

Someone who can get a walkie-talkie to you if we can get our hands on them. They don't need to be a fighter, just very fast." Fawke peered over the rim of his cup.

"I have just the person. A youngster named Roland. Fast as a deer, lithe, knows the area well. He'll find us once we move on." He snapped his fingers for the woman who'd brought our food to fetch the boy.

She returned a few minutes later with a dark-skinned boy of around twelve or thirteen years of age. He stared at us with wide eyes.

"Relax, son," Jenkins said. "You're going on a mission with these people. Hopefully, not for long." He explained what would be required of the boy. "Can you do this?"

Roland squared his shoulders. "Like taking milk from a baby."

"It'll be dangerous," I said, ducking my head to hide a smile at his bravado.

"I'm not afraid."

"You should be," Fawke said. "Only fools venture out there without fear. Are you a fool?"

The boy's eyes widened. "No, sir."

"Good." Fawke returned to his meal. "Get some rest. We leave at first light."

"Please keep the boy safe. He shows great promise at being a fine warrior someday. He's been training with the others." Jenkins crossed his arms and leaned back in his chair, the wood creaking under his weight.

"I promise to do my best." Fawke wiped his mouth on the back of his hand. "Knowing he has some skill with a weapon will work in his favor."

"You wouldn't happen to have that radio, Sharon uses, would you?" Jenkins steepled his fingers.

"You know her?" Surprise leaped in me.

"We have a…history, her and I." He exhaled heavily through his nose. "The radio would give me a means of communicating with her."

"Why?" What kind of a game was he playing?

He shrugged. "Keep your enemies close as they say. She knows we've survived. Why not find out exactly what she knows?"

"You actually think she'll tell you?" Fawke's voice hardened. "What kind of history was between the two of you?"

"We were best friends. Her father was my father's best friend, but refused to live in these mountains. He took his family back to the city to beg the president for mercy." A muscle twitched in his jaw. "I believe strongly in bringing Soriah to its knees."

That was the last thing I'd expected him to say. The trust I'd started feeling toward him trickled away. That kind of secret should have been brought upfront in the beginning. "No, we left the radio behind. How did you know such a thing exists?"

"Because one was brought with those who fled Soriah in order to keep in contact, if they needed to. I often thought they had allies left behind. As far as I know, those who fled never used it."

After we ate, we rounded up those who had stayed behind. They weren't happy to leave the safety of their new home.

"I'm starting a new life here," Samson said, his

arm around a pretty woman. "I don't want to die out there."

"If we don't stop the army, there won't be anything to come back to." I narrowed my eyes. "Can we count on you?"

He glanced at the woman at his side. "Yes. If it means her safety."

"You aren't the only one leaving someone behind." Lotus glared. "We've all formed relationships here. Not to go, to fight for their safety, means they could perish. We don't have a choice."

I widened my eyes. The girl had once been our weakest fighter. To have grown a strong spine now would benefit us all. "I'm glad to see you'll come without orders."

"We've continued our training while helping others," Riva added. "We can do what needs to be done."

"Good." I nodded. "Rest up, make sure you have what you need, and say your goodbyes. I don't know how long we'll be gone. Moses, I put the young boy, Roland, under your care. Protect him."

"Will do. What if we come across others out there?"

The question I'd dreaded. "They have the choice of joining us or dying. We can't chance them returning to Soriah." I turned and marched to the training ring to watch those I'd choose the five fighters from. I wanted those who could get the job done, but wouldn't take the best from Jenkins. This community would need able fighters. What I wanted were those who could fight and follow orders enough to be an asset.

Fawke joined me, folding his arms on the rail of the ring. "I'm glad you aren't leaving any of our people behind."

"I can't. We need them. We're still going to be grossly outnumbered. How many scouts, scavengers, army personnel are out there now? Way more than the twenty plus that make up our group."

"If we keep surprise on our side, staying out of sight as much as possible, striking when they aren't expecting…we have a chance, Crynn. A good one. Besides, who wouldn't want to leave the tyranny of Soriah?"

I faced him. "Back to always being optimistic?" I thought back to how angry he'd been when the choice of returning to Soriah had been taken away from him. With less than two years to go, his time as a Stalker had almost been paid. He'd have returned to live a life of luxury.

He rolled his neck on his shoulders. "I was an idiot to think I'd prefer life under the rule of President Cane rather than live free among the trees." He glanced upward. "The air is fresher here, the sky seems less dark. The earth is trying to heal herself. That won't happen as long as Soriah keeps its people packed into a city as crowded as a box of matches."

"I'm glad you feel that way," I said softly.

He cupped my cheek. "I wouldn't have been able to leave you behind. Surely you know that."

"I'd hoped you couldn't." I leaned into his touch.

"Hey, you two." Dante rushed toward us. "Mind coming and seeing what supplies Jenkins has said he can spare? Make sure it's enough?"

Stepping away from Fawke, I nodded. Without

knowing how long we'd be gone, we'd need a lot of supplies. Until we could get the walkie-talkies, we wouldn't be able to ask for more.

A third wagon, filled with crates of food and water joined the two we'd dragged back with us. Those two held more supplies.

Kira rummaged through a box of medical supplies.

Moses studied a pile of weapons, swords mostly, but an extra gun or two. "We really need to find this arsenal. We're leaving these people shorthanded."

"Give back what you think we can spare." We all carried our weapons on us. Hopefully, anyone we ran across would be armed. Strange thing to hope for. Armed people were dangerous, but whether they joined us or not, we'd have more, by force if necessary. It would have to be enough.

"Are you sure?" Moses frowned.

"We can't take what they will need." I strolled around the wagons. Tents, blankets, food, weapons…we could do this. All we had to do was find a base camp not easily located. One where the supplies could be kept when the group ventured out to search for the hidden arsenal. If it existed at all.

The army could have been sent not to search for the weapons, but to hunt the rebels. If we could get our hands on a tank or two…

"If you run across any scavengers," a woman called out, "we could stand to have a few luxuries here."

"We'll do our best." I chuckled, the mood lightened. "No sense letting Soriah get richer."

"This looks good." Fawke's gaze roamed over

the wagons. "We sure will be loaded down, though. I prefer moving quickly."

"We'll find a camp. Somewhere on the outskirts. Moses, the map."

He spread it on top of the supplies. "This would work. An abandoned amusement park. If memory serves me right from the history books, the workers stayed in underground bunkers. We'd be protected, as long as Malignants haven't claimed the place."

"If they have, we'll clear them out. It's nothing we haven't done before. How many days to get there?"

He shrugged. "Three maybe. It's on the far side of the city, but we might not have to go through. Hopefully, we can stay on the outskirts, away from the army, and arrive undetected."

I glanced at each face in my group. "I'll go choose the five who will join our ranks." Tomorrow, we head out to face a greater opponent than we'd seen before.

I chose five nineteen-year-olds, figuring they'd be more physically fit than older people. Maybe less experienced at life, but more trainable. I'd do my best to make sure they returned to their families.

No promises were made. The danger too great to expect us all to return.

4

It took four days to reach the amusement park. Four days of pulling wagons, removing debris, and taking shelter from the rain. Not all of us had rubber suits to protect us so we'd huddle under any overhang or empty building that would hold us. Finally, I stood under a leaning Ferris wheel, minus half its cars, and waited for Moses and Ezra to find the entrance to the underground bunkers.

The newest five to join our ranks had trudge with us without complaints, pulling their weight clearing a path for the wagons. I'd chosen well in choosing young. I smiled. They were all a year older than myself, yet I felt as old as Ezra a lot of the time.

"Here." Moses tossed aside a flat piece of sheet metal. It clanged against an iron railing. "If anyone is inside, they didn't get in this way."

"We need to find all entrances and kill some Malignants." I hopped off the stack of rubble I'd stood on to scout the area.

"What?" Soran, one of our new, frowned. "You want to actually go looking for them?"

"They hide our scent. We place them at the entrances." I marched to the entrance and peered into the darkness. No foul smell of death greeted me. I think we got lucky. "Stay alert. Fawke and I will go below first."

"You know, leaders in history always sent in the grunts first," Ezra said.

I laughed. "I don't send anyone to do what I'm not willing to. If something happens to us, you're in charge." I lit a lantern and held it high before descending the cement stairs.

The air smelled dank, a hint of mildew, but not the putrid stench of Malignants. Decades of dust muffled our footprints as we descended.

A long hallway with rooms branching in both directions lured us to investigate further. If we could find another exit, one we could use to escape if we were found, we'd have our place of refuge. At least temporarily.

Faded paint on walls in different corridors stretched in every direction directing those who had once wandered these halls so they could find their way. Gas powered vehicles, long left abandoned rested in alcoves.

"There's a whole city under here," I whispered.

"Why the whisper?" Fawke grinned.

"Just seemed right." How many children had enjoyed the park overhead without having an inkling of what lay below? "Do you think there's anything of value down here?"

"Besides a place to live that's free of monsters? I don't know. But this place was built like a fortress. There's bound to be something. It seems as if it was meant to help humans survive."

As we moved along the corridor, large pipes and cables increased overhead. Hope leaped in me. What if there was gas? Food preserved for such a time as this? We could hide an army in these halls and rooms.

We glanced into a large control room with computers and monitors that no longer worked. A few doors down we located a dining room with stainless-steel tables and chairs. I spotted a kitchen through a door across the room. Further exploration revealed rooms where the park's employees had lived. Steel cots with moth-eaten blankets, chests with remnants of costumes no longer useful.

"There has to be a storage room," I said. "If there are useful things to be found, they'll be there."

"Let's get the others. We can start bringing our supplies in and store them in the dining room," Fawke said. "We can explore faster with more people."

I nodded and headed back the way we'd come. At the bottom of the steps, I called, "Bring down the supplies, then hide the wagons. We've found our camp."

"Erase any evidence of our presence," Fawke added.

It took more than an hour for the supplies to be brought in.

"This place is great." Kira glanced around, grinning. "I bet there's an infirmary. Any medicines will have gone bad by now, but if I can clean the place up, it will give me a place to treat the injured."

"We'll leave that to you. Take Gage with you to

locate the room." I directed the others to the dining room, watching with satisfaction as our supplies found a home. "There are plenty of rooms to choose as your new home. For the first time in a long time, you'll enjoy some privacy. Once you've done that, meet back here so we can form teams to further explore this place."

I set off to the first available dormitory and tossed my pack on the cot. Home, strange as it was. Once cleaned of dirt and cobwebs, I'd be quite comfortable there.

"I'm right across the hall." Fawke leaned in the doorway. "Figured you choose the first room so anyone passing through would have to get by you first."

I laughed. "You know me so well. How many rats do you think are in this place?"

"Thousands." He grinned. "As long as we lock up any food, they'll leave us alone. The others are already gathering for the meeting. Ready?"

With one last look at my new home, I followed him back to the dining room where everyone sat, attention on me. I assigned teams to clean and stock the kitchen, others to explore the large expanse of rooms for anything of value. Fawke and I would continue searching for another exit. If we found more than one, we'd board them up so no one could sneak up on us unaware. "Bring anything you think we can use back to this room. If it can be repaired, we can use it."

I jerked my head toward the door for Fawke to follow, confident the others would do as I'd asked. We moved quickly past the area we'd already explored and turned right at what seemed to be the center of the complex. Halls radiated out like a wagon wheel. We turned right down the first one.

Each door led to an office. At the end of the hall, a heavy steel door led to a fallen down building that allowed no access without clearing a ton of debris. No need to block that exit.

We continued along the same vein finally coming to a large room full of crates and metal chests. *Please, let there be supplies*. Dried foods, anything to help us face the battle ahead.

Fawke located a crowbar and started prying open crates. Tools, thread-bare blankets, cans of paint thick as mud. "There has to be food somewhere. The darkness that descended upon the world didn't come as a surprise. Why put this much trouble in maintaining such a place if a person didn't plan on trying to survive down here?"

"What do you think happened to these people? After the closing of the park?"

He shrugged. "Died of old age, maybe. It was a hundred years ago."

"You actually think they'd have found a way to preserve food and water for that long?"

"Someone would have wanted to keep the human race going." He opened all the crates before moving to the metal chests. The first one opened with a hiss. A freezing mist escaped. A grin spread across his face. "Bingo."

"If that's the case," I peered down to see packets of what I could only assume was food, "then I bet there's gas for those vehicles. Don't you think this is too easy?"

"Possibly, but no way the rubber gaskets would be any good after all this time. As for easy, I welcome easy for once." He handed me a packet. "Mashed potatoes?"

Tears clogged my throat. Maybe we could win this fight after all. Thanks to the brains of past scientists who prepared for the danger encroaching on the world, we had a chance.

Fawke wrapped his arms around me. "We're going to be okay. We've found a safe place with food. I bet there's weapons here that Ezra can clean and make work."

"Ancient weapons." I choked back a half sob, half laugh. "What if there are unfriendlies that won't relish newcomers."

"Ancient is better than nothing. Maybe the army won't know what's shooting at them." His chest vibrated with silent laughter. "Let's finish these crates and have a few days rest before we tackle what's ahead. Done worry about what we don't know."

I nodded, stepping back. "We can make one of these rooms a place to train. Think of how many people we can house here if we find others willing to fight with us."

By the time we'd finished opening the crates, we'd discovered enough food to last us for months if we could get the refrigerator in the kitchen to work. The packets would need to stay frozen. No weapons, though, but there was still a lot of compound to explore.

The further we moved through the place, the more we found. Gas for lanterns. Fawke was right about the vehicles. I doubted they'd ever run again. We blocked off doors as we went, saving the furthest one as our escape route. A door that came out under what had once been a man-made waterfall, now dry.

"If we mark our way with a signal only our people will know, if anyone infiltrates this place, we'll know which way to run, leaving them lost." At least that was my hope. "Do you remember the way back?"

He nodded and picked up a piece of wood. He lit it, blackening the end. "We'll mark the way with a C on each corner. It won't be obvious to anyone looking. We'll have a few practice runs to make sure everyone can find their way out. No more work today." He led the way back to the dining room, leaving marks as we went.

Ezra greeted us with a grin. "We actually found some blankets and mattresses that while old, are serviceable."

"We found food." I handed him the packet of freeze-dried potatoes. "If you can get that refrigerator working, it'll last us a good long while."

"I'll find a way to make it work." He hugged the packet to his chest like the treasure it was.

Kira joined us. "The infirmary is in good shape. No medicines though. We'll have to make do with what Jenkins supplied us with, but it's something."

I'd never been more optimistic about our future. "Good job, everyone. Tonight, and tomorrow, we do nothing but rest. No fighting. No training. Then, we prepare for war."

A shout came from outside the room. I unsheathed my sword and turned.

Dante and Moses escorted an elderly man with a bowed back, leaning heavily on an aluminum cane, into the room. "Meet Eb, age ninety-nine. The man who has kept this place up."

"It's been a long time since I've seen another living soul," Eb said, sitting in a chair Dante pulled out for him. "I hid when I heard your group coming, but this young man found me and convinced me that I could be of service to you."

I held out my hand. "Crynn Dayholt, sir, and the pleasure is all mine. Your service will be invaluable." Someone who had survived this long outside of Soriah could be our greatest find yet.

5

"Forget everything you think you know about this world." He tapped his cane on the floor, the sound echoing in the room. "Because you're wrong."

I pulled up a chair and sat across from him. "Have you been here your whole life?"

He nodded. "I was born here. My parents fled Soriah when my mother was pregnant with me. They saw what was coming."

"How is that possible?" I glanced at Fawke, doing the math in my head. "The bombs fell over a hundred years ago."

"No!" He banged his cane again. "Listen to me. Forget what you were told. The bombs didn't come for twenty-five years after the day my parents stepped foot in this place. They came with fifty others, all long dead, except for a few that ventured out. The park employees were here, making their number in the hundreds. I'm the last. I've done my best to keep this place up, praying for other refugees."

"Have you not ventured outside once?" How could he not want to know what had happened?

"Why? The monitors in the control room work. I watched it all. Felt the ground shake as the bombs fell. Watched people left in the open turn into monsters. I've had no need to go out there." He closed his eyes for a second before continuing.

"The nations of the world didn't blow each other up. Soriah did. The president at that time, Cane, I suppose it's his heir that runs things now, wanted complete reign. So," he shrugged, "he destroyed everything outside of what is behind those white walls. My father was a commander in his army and wanted no part of what was to come."

"So, he fled." Ice dripped from Ezra's words. "Like a coward instead of slitting Cane's throat while he had the chance."

"Hoping to find a way to stop Cane. Don't be an idiot. One doesn't simply walk up to the president and assassinate him. Instead, my father died down here like all the rest trying to find a way." He lifted dark eyes to mine. "It's up to you now to stop this tyranny."

"Did anyone get out of here?"

"A handful fled." He shrugged. "No one knows whether they survived."

I smiled and told him of the Rebel City, the army, the wheel... "We're here to put an end to this."

Hope brightened his wrinkled face. "Let me show you how to watch the world from the safety of this place."

"We can't stay locked up. We have to stop the army."

He nodded, using the cane to get to his feet. "That's my hope. Get rid of the army, then infiltrate Soriah. Finish off Cane and this nightmare stops." He led the way slowly down the hall, pressing his hand against a panel on the wall.

A door slid open, revealing another room. "This is the real control room. The other ran the park. From here, you can watch it all."

He pressed some buttons on a keyboard. Monitors flickered to life, filling one entire wall.

In the distance I could make out the towers of Soriah, the mountain where Rebel City thrived, the burning city. Everything. I grinned and glanced at Fawke before turning my attention back to Eb. "Tell me you have weapons."

"Do I ever." He laughed and shuffled to a wall opposite the monitors. Another hidden panel revealed an arsenal. "It takes an army to fight an army. My father planned well. For too many years, no one could leave this place because of the radiation. After another twenty years, those I told you about took their chances, not wanting to spend their life underground."

"Do you know a man named Jenkins?"

"I knew a Jenkins as a child. Why?"

"He's the leader of the rebels." I frowned. "He said he had a relationship with Sharon, the current president's right hand. How is that possible? If she had been here, she would know the location of this place."

"Not necessarily. She was nothing more than a child. When my father located this compound, he brought the others here blindfolded. When the others wanted to leave, they were escorted out the same way. This Sharon must have fled back to the city with her family. No one knows the location of this place, only that it exists."

"This is what the army is looking for. This place, these weapons." I swallowed against a dry throat. Jenkins also knows this place exists. He no longer lived here, but kept the fact it existed secret, knowing we'd find a way. The man had put a lot of faith in us.

"We need to get everything back up and running," Ezra said. "If we're to make this our base, we'll need the food and supplies."

"You'll never run out of food. This place is infested with rats. I eat them all the time." Eb laughed. "Saves the freeze-dried meals for another time."

Nausea churned in my stomach. "Just rats?"

"Don't be silly. They're just the protein, although I do have beans." He pressed another button on the keyboard, changing one of the monitors to a room full of light. "A garden such as you've never seen. I told you my father planned well, bringing seeds from many varieties. Keeping the garden going is what keeps me going. How do you think the vegetables got in those metal crates? Oh, yes, I watched you from these monitors until I deemed you trustworthy. Then, I stepped out and that's when the young man found me."

This was a lot to take in. I leaned against the wall. "You always knew someone would come."

"Of course. I've seen you people jumping from helicopters. Wasn't sure why, but…" He shrugged. "Never would have guessed you'd spun a wheel.

Barbaric way to determine a person's future. Another way for Soriah to lord it over everyone."

"Are there medical supplies?"

"No. Couldn't keep them from spoiling, but I guarantee the army will have some."

True. The problem would be getting to them without being killed. The arsenal behind the wall helped even the odds. "Vehicles?"

"Nope. Couldn't keep them going. I'm not much of a mechanic."

Oh, well. We'd been on foot for a long time. We'd continue that way.

After a brief lesson on using the monitors, Eb declared himself exhausted and went to his room. I assigned the task of watching the monitors to Lars and Dayton, telling them to work in shifts. We wouldn't leave them unattended for one minute. "Alert me if you see any movement."

"Will do." Lars took first shift, leaving Dayton to head to his room to get sleep.

The rest of us congregated in the dining room.

"This place is unbelievable," Gage said, folding her arms on a table. "I mean, Ezra suspected an arsenal, but an entire compound?" She shook her head. "I can see why no one would want to leave this place."

"We have to." I sat across from her. "We have a job to do."

"I know." She took a deep breath. "I'll go help Riva with our meal."

Over the next few weeks, Eb watched as we honed our fighting skills, pored over maps of the city, and formulated a plan of attack. We had the element of surprise on our side. By now, the army might have believed we'd perished at the claws of Malignants.

We grew stronger, not only in skill, but physically, eating three meals a day of beans and vegetables or rats and vegetables. I'd force down the rats, knowing I needed the nourishment, and kept my mind from dwelling on the fact I ate a rodent. Rodents that came from the outside.

"Crynn?" Lars voice came over the loudspeaker. "We've got a runner."

I thundered down the hall to the control room and peered over his shoulder. A man in army fatigues sprinted toward us, four Malignants on his heels. "How'd he get separated from the rest?"

"Who cares?" Fawke grabbed a sword off the wall. "We can't leave him out there."

"We've got a jail cell," Eb said, joining us. "You can keep him there until we know if he can be trusted."

Nodding, I grabbed a sword of my own. A gun would only alert the army that we were still in the city.

"Use this." Eb pulled an earpiece from a drawer. "We can communicate with you while you're out there. Let you know if anyone is close."

"Thanks." I slipped the piece in my ear and followed Fawke to the entrance under the Ferris Wheel. "If he sees us, we can't let him escape."

"Then let's make sure we catch him." He ascended the steps and opened the door.

Outside, we headed in the direction of the runner. At the sight of us, he skidded to a stop.

"Get behind us, fool." Fawke held his sword

ready.

I did the same, taking off the head of the first malignant to get too close. The soldier's scream distracted me. I turned a fraction to see why. Another malignant's claws raked across my ribcage, before I plunged my sword into its gut.

My mid-section burned as if someone had poured acid on me. "I'm cut." How had I allowed myself to be so careless as to get too close?

Fawke finished off the last one and faced me, his features stern. "Let's get back. Kira needs to clean that wound."

"You're the rebels." The soldier staggered back a few feet, reaching for the gun on his belt that wasn't there, proving we most likely couldn't trust him.

"Yeah, the ones that saved your sorry ass." Fawke held the tip of his sword to the man's throat. "Turn around. Crynn, your scarf."

I unwound it from my neck and tied it around the soldier's hands. I used another strip of fabric from my clothes to blindfold him.

"Where are you taking me?" His voice squeaked.

"Just walk." Fawke poked him.

We didn't remove the blindfold until we reached the jail cell. Fawke whipped it off, untied the man's hands, and shoved him into the cell.

Eb shuffled forward and locked the door. "Glad you thought of the blindfold."

"It worked for your father." Fawke smiled. "Kira, tend to Crynn. She's been wounded."

Legs weak now that the adrenaline had worn off, I nodded, leaning heavily on her. "Malignant claws."

"You're lucky you weren't bit. We couldn't save

41

you then." She helped me to the infirmary and onto a bed. "As it is, you'll feel like you're dying for a few days." She cut away my shirt, revealing three gashes already turning green. "Nasty. Lay still. Keep your heart rate as slow as possible."

She turned to some supplies on a rolling table and poured something into a glass. She handed it to me. "Drink this. It will help with the pain. Best do it in one gulp."

I wrinkled my nose at the odor of sulfur, then downed the medicine. "Oh. Gross." My stomach rebelled.

"Do not throw up. It's worse the second time." She laughed.

"This is not funny." I narrowed my eyes.

"Lay back and get ready."

"For what?"

"For the fire of hell." She poured something else over my wound.

I arched my back and screamed.

6

Dreams plagued my sleep. Nightmares of bombs and Malignants. Sharon's face hovered behind my eyelids, laughing, promising my head on a stake as an example to anyone foolish enough to join the rebels. A horde of monsters leaped on Fawke, ripping him to shreds. I screamed and opened my eyes.

"It's okay." Fawke put a hand on each of my shoulders, his touch calming me. "Kira, she's burning up."

"Here." She thrust a bowl into his hands. "Cool her down with this."

He mopped my face with a rag dampened with cool water. "It was just a dream."

"You were being torn apart." My gaze searched his face.

"I'm fine." He smiled, worry creasing his forehead. "Worry about yourself."

"Very funny. How long have I been here?"

"Three days. This is the first you've been conscious." He moved the rag to my neck, the coolness soothing.

"The prisoner?"

"Locked up and being taken care of. Stop worrying. Focus on getting well."

My eyes closed. When I woke again, I found myself alone, sweating, tangled in my blankets. On the table next to my bed sat another dose of the foul medicine. I forced it down, then sat up, waiting for my head to stop spinning.

"You shouldn't be up." Mariah entered the room with a tray. "Hungry?"

"Actually, I am. Where's Kira?"

"Sleeping. I've brought you some broth."

I wrinkled my nose, knowing it came from yet another rodent. "How long did I sleep this time?"

"Only a few hours. Can you manage or shall I feed you?"

"I can manage." No way did I want to be fed like an infant. I wasn't that helpless.

She set the bowl of broth on the rolling table and moved it in front of me. "I'll be back in a few minutes to check on you. Fawke wants to know the minute you wake up."

"Let him sleep. I'll talk to him in the morning." Already, my body cried out for more rest. "I'll drink this and go back to sleep."

The next time I woke, Fawke sat in a chair beside my bed. "Your fever broke." He smiled.

I sat up, relieved to be on the mend. I glanced at the fresh bandages around my ribcage. "I'd like to talk to the prisoner now."

"It can wait. The others are pleased you're going to survive."

"No more than I am." Although, I'd thought differently the first day. "Anything of concern happen while I was down?"

"The monitors spotted some Malignants, a couple of soldiers scouting the area, but nothing to be alarmed about. This place is well hidden. Not even the nose of a monster can sniff us out."

"This place is too good to be true."

"Eb has survived here a very long time. We're safe." He took my hand, his thumb rubbing the top of mine.

"I keep waiting for it to all cave in on us."

"That's the illness talking."

I sat up and swung my legs over the side of the bed. "Let's interrogate the prisoner. I'll take it easy. I promise." The room spun a bit as I stood, but settled.

Leaning on Fawke, we made our way to the cell.

The prisoner gripped the bars. "How long are you going to keep me here?"

I sat in a chair outside the cell. "You can't leave."

"So, I'm a prisoner."

"You were going to shoot us."

"I was scared. I'd just been chased by those things." He shoved against the bar and paced his cell. "I wasn't thinking straight. What is this place?"

"Our camp. Where is the army?"

Shrugging, he sat on his bunk, his hands dangling between his knees. "I don't know. I got separated from them, then ran across those things, lost my gun." He shook his head. "I didn't want to be a soldier. I wanted to be a baker."

"But the wheel chose differently." I sighed.

"Yeah. Let me stay here. I can help."

"You don't even know where the other soldiers are." I arched a brow. "How can you help us?"

"You find the army. I'll go in and spy for you."

"Or tell them about us." It would take a while for me to be convinced we could trust him. Without some information from him that would help us succeed with our mission, we couldn't.

"I promise. I don't want that job. Let me work in your kitchen." He returned to the bars, gripping them hard enough to turn his knuckles white. "What can I do to make you trust me?"

"I'll let you know." I motioned to Fawke that I was ready to leave. "The dining room, please." In the hall, I asked, "Who's been feeding him?"

"Lotus."

"Then, I'd like to speak with her."

We sat at a table away from the others. "Has the prisoner said anything to you?" I asked her.

"His name is Jobe. He's nothing but a grunt, in charge of digging latrines. Nice though." She shrugged. "As to where the army is, all he's mentioned is that they're outside of the city."

"Any mention of the mountain or why they're here?"

"Looking for rebels. Orders to kill on sight." Concern flickered in her eyes. "He seems nice. Nothing more than a scared young man out of his element."

Scared people could sometimes be the most dangerous. "Do you trust him?"

"I'm a former criminal accused of murder." She laughed. "I don't trust anyone other than this group."

It was hard to picture the pretty, petite girl as a cold-blooded killer. When Soriah had sent her, she'd barely been able to fight.

"Do you think you can get him to talk?"

She gave a coy smile. "I can get a man to do anything. If he knows something that will help us, you'll know soon enough."

I laughed. "I leave him in your very capable hands."

After the noon meal, I was more than ready for a nap. Fawke took me to my own room this time, promising to return in a couple of hours. "Good. I'd like to watch the monitors for a while." The army was out there. Maybe I'd see something to help us find them.

True to his word, Fawke woke me in two hours, a cup of the foul medicine in his hand. "You aren't out of danger of infection yet. Drink up."

"I hate this stuff." I closed my eyes and downed it, shuddering. "The next time I let myself get distracted, clobber me."

"Could've been worse. A lot worse. If you'd gotten bitten, I'd have had to kill you. That would have been the end of me," he said softly. "I hope this place doesn't make us soft."

"As soon as I'm able, we'll take a team out. Doing so will help keep our senses alert." I stood slowly and marched to the control room, glad to see Eb there. I hadn't seen him in the days I'd been ill. At his age, I worried.

"Glad you're up and about young lady. All is boring on this front."

I sat in the chair next to him. "No sign of

anything?"

"Just those things. There's a lot more of them than I used to see. Something has them stirred up."

I glanced back at Fawke. "The army?"

"Or they followed our scent here when we brought the soldier."

"They can't get in," Eb said, "but they can make your leaving more difficult."

"No way to lure them away?"

"I've a siren, but that would draw the army, too. Best to just wait them out."

"What's the siren for?" Fawke asked.

"The only time it went off was when the bombs fell."

If I had a bomb, I'd drop it on the city to rid it of Malignants and spend the rest of my days safe in the compound. But, that would be the coward way out and wouldn't stop Soriah. "Fine. We wait for them to move away. By then, I'll be ready to go on the hunt."

The next morning, Lotus didn't show for breakfast. Fawke and I checked her room before heading to the jail cell.

Her body lay inside, the soldier gone.

"Find him," I ordered, kneeling beside Lotus. Her head lay an odd angle, her neck broken. Why had she gone inside?

Anger rolled in waves. "Bring him to me."

The others dashed away, heading down each hall of the compound.

Fawke scooped Lotus into his arms. "I'll take her to the infirmary until we decide what to do with her body. Eb must have disposed of those who've died somehow."

One of our own, nothing more than something to be gotten rid of. My hands curled into fists as I marched back to the dining room to await the prisoner being brought to me. He couldn't have escaped the compound. Lars would've seen him on the monitors.

I paced the room, holding my arm tight against my wounded side. I'd kill him. Tears burned my eyes at Lotus's senseless death.

"I burn the bodies," Eb said, coming up behind me. "The smoke from the incinerator blends with the smoke from the city."

The incinerator where the garbage is tossed. I whirled as Dante and Ezra shoved Jobe into the room.

"Why?" My voice thundered.

"To escape." His gaze hardened. Standing before me was a soldier, not a frightened young man. Quite the actor, this one. "Unfortunately, I couldn't find my way out."

"For that, you'll die."

He lifted his chin. "So be it."

A cruel smile twisted my lips. "Oh, you won't be so brave in a few minutes. Tie his hands, blindfold him, and toss him out."

"You're handing me to those things with no means of defending myself?"

"Lotus had no way of defending herself against you." I turned my back to him and headed to the control room where I pulled up the camera that showed our main entrance.

Ezra opened the door and shoved Jobe out.

The soldier stood still, apparently listening

before taking a stumbling run away from the door. Shrieks came from the rubble as Malignants darted forward. Soon, Jobe's screams joined their shrieks.

"Brutal way to kill someone," Lars said hoarsely.

"He snapped Lotus's neck like a twig."

"Then good riddance. What now? Those things won't leave until they learn no more food will come out that door."

"We wait." I pushed to my feet, turning my face away from the look on young Roland's face, and back to my room. With a groan, I stretched out on my bed, exhaustion weighing me down.

A knock sounded at the door. "Come in."

Fawke entered. "You alright?"

"It's not easy ordering someone's death." I turned my face to the wall, ashamed of the decision I'd been forced to make. "Leave me alone, please."

"Kira wants to put clean bandages on your wound."

"Tell her to wait. I'm going to sleep."

"Crynn—"

"Go."

His footsteps moved away. The door creaked as he closed it.

I let the tears I'd held in fall. Not for the man I'd ordered killed, but for Lotus. I'd asked her to get information from the man. That had caused her death. How would I explain to the man she'd left behind in Rebel City that she died because of something I'd asked her to do?

I didn't know how long I lay there in misery before heading to the infirmary. Without speaking, I sat on the bed and let Kira tend to my dressing.

As if sensing my mood, she kept silent, cleaning and redressing the gashes in my side. When she finished, I headed back to the control room, intending to sit there until I found out something that would tell us where the army waited.

7

After another week, the Malignants had moved far enough away that we deemed it safe to venture outside. Fawke, Ezra, Dante, and myself prepared to head out. I slipped the earpiece in my ear and turned to Lars. "Keep in contact. You're our eyes out there."

"Will do."

"I want to go." Roland, a sword hanging from his thin hips, stood in the doorway.

"No. You're too valuable. Once we get those walkie-talkies, you'll be headed back to the mountain."

"I need more training." A belligerent look crossed his face.

"I said no." Aware of my harsh tone, I sighed. What had happened to the nice Crynn Dayholt? "We promised Jenkins. When it's time, we'll escort you out of the city and let you return to your family." I put a hand on his shoulder. "Not much longer, I promise. I'm sure Lars could use another set of eyes on the monitors. Would you mind?"

"I'm not a baby."

"Dude. This is the most important job here." Lars waved him forward. "It's up to us to keep them safe. I really could use a fresh set of eyes."

Fawke bent, meeting the boy's gaze head on. "I'm depending on you. Last time, Crynn was injured. Without eyes in here, one of us might die."

Placated, the boy nodded. "I can do this." He plopped into a chair and stared at the monitors, putting a headset over his kinky hair.

"I feel safer already." I smiled and led the way to our main entrance. We needed to get Roland back to Rebel City before he did something rash.

We stopped just outside the door. I cringed as it banged closed, expecting to be attacked. "Tell us which way, guys."

"Go to your right," Roland said. "I see movement that way. Dust. That could mean jeeps about a mile away."

"Good job." I turned to Fawke. "Have you noticed there's been no newcomers? Not one mention of a chopper or a parachute. Does that mean Soriah stopped the wheel spinning or has no one gotten unlucky?"

"Maybe we haven't seen anything on the monitors. If there are more stalkers, we'll find them."

Not unless the army did first. We moved with caution away from the compound.

"Stop." Roland's voice came through the earpiece. "Monsters coming."

After a few minutes, Roland told us to continue. What a great way to make a bored teenager feel valued. I was certain Lars told him what to tell us, but knowing the boy was occupied and safe eased my worry for him.

"You've got a group of people one block over. Not soldiers. Looks like six or seven."

"Scouts?"

"Maybe. Proceed with caution."

Fawke chuckled. "His vocabulary has improved."

I grinned and followed him as he sprinted across the street and down an alley. We stopped at the sound of hushed voices. I glanced over my shoulder at Ezra and Dante, motioning for them to circle around. With only four of us, surprise was our best bet at not getting killed.

"They've a hostage," Dante spoke through the earpiece. "A girl. Most likely a new stalker."

"Move in," I said. "Don't let her be a casualty." The rest of the group, all men, looked rough, strong. I'd bet they were released criminals sent to help find us. "We do not take the men with us."

"You want us to kill them?" Ezra asked.

"If we have to. Otherwise, disarm and tie up. Use your guns. Go."

"You want to risk the noise?" Fawke arched a brow.

"Much bigger threat than swords." I stepped into the open as the others did the same, circling the group gathered around a fire. "Hello."

"Well, look at you. We thought there was only one little girl out here all alone." A man with a full beard leered.

"Not alone, boss," another said. "She's got three armed men with her."

He made a move for his gun propped against a wall.

"I wouldn't if I were you." I aimed my weapon at his chest. "Move away from the weapons and the girl."

"Or what?" His features hardened.

"I shoot you." I grinned.

"You're the rebels we were sent to find." His eyes widened as the real threat of danger occurred to him.

"Maybe. What are you? A released prisoner?"

"Smart girl."

"We have a few of our own. Men with nothing to lose." I motioned for Ezra and Dante to collect their weapons. "Shall we kill you or leave you to try and find the army to protect you?"

"You can't leave us unarmed!"

"You can keep your swords. Dante, the girl."

He nodded and moved to untie her, keeping his body between her and the men.

"Let's compete for the guns." Boss Man said. "I fight your strongest. If I win, we take your weapons and the girl. If you win, the same goes to you."

I rubbed a hand over my face. "I'm the strongest, and I'm too tired to play games."

His laugh rang out.

A shriek rose from the other side of the building.

"Time to go," Fawke said.

"You've got seven of those things coming at full speed in your direction," Roland said. "Get out of there."

We whirled. I shouted for the other group to run. From the sound of pounding feet, they followed my order, fleeing in the opposite direction.

"The monsters split up. You've got four coming your way," Roland said. "The other three went after those men."

"Circle up" Fawke shoved the girl in the center as the rest of us drew our swords, ready to fight.

Adrenaline burned through me as I remembered the last time I'd faced these monsters. I stood at the ready, determined not to lose focus this time. I ignored the whimpers of the girl behind me and lunged.

The stench of Malignant blood filled the air as my sword plunged into its heart. I ripped up, then slashed upward as another leaped into the air. My sword impaled it, driving us both to the ground. Its teeth snapped next to my face. This was it. The day I died.

A well-placed boot bashed in its head. I stared into the pale face of the girl we'd rescued. "Thanks." I shoved the dead beast off me.

She nodded, then fainted.

"At least she isn't a coward." Fawke held out a blood-covered hand to help me to my feet.

"Lucky for me. Are these things getting stronger or am I losing my touch?" I wiped my hands on my clothes.

"We aren't keeping up on our training. Staying safe in the compound has us weak." He glanced around the area. "Talk to us."

"Area looks clear." Roland's voice shook. "I thought Crynn was a goner."

"Not yet," I said. "Eyes on the army?"

"No, but those men you encountered are coming

back."

I groaned. "Let's not be here when they arrive. Let's continue to the last sighting of where the army was. Wake her up." I jerked my head toward the unconscious girl.

Dante patted her face until her eyes opened. "Come on, wilting violet. We've got to go." He hauled her to her feet and handed her one of the extra swords. "Hope you know how to use this."

"Not really."

"Learn fast."

We darted up the road, skirting around debris, following the directions given to us by Roland. I could hear Lars giving instruction to him occasionally.

"Jeeps! Straight ahead." This time Lars spoke directly to us. "They're following those men."

Darn it. The men had escaped the Malignants and told the army about us. "We can't fight them."

"We'll have to hide." Fawke raced for a building.

Inside, we plastered our backs to the pitted concrete wall and switched our swords for guns. I cradled mine to my chest and peered out a broken window as first the men who'd had the girl sprinted past, then a jeep rumbled by. A man stood behind a machine gun. Another had a pair of binoculars to his eyes and scanned the road.

"Where's the other jeep?" I asked.

"The other side of the building," Roland said. "You're surrounded."

"Who are you people?" The girl sat on what was left of a chair, eyes wide in her pale face. Red curls tumbled around her shoulders.

"Soriah's worst enemy." Dante's teeth flashed against his dark skin. "What's your name?"

"Rory. Those men grabbed me before I could get myself out of my chute."

"Let's save the conversation for later." I kept my attention on the soldiers outside.

A shriek came from a floor above us. Oh, God. We were taking refuge among Malignants. If they charged, they'd give us away. We couldn't fight without the army finding us. I put a finger to my mouth, hoping the blood from our previous fight would disguise our scent.

I jerked my head toward a hallway. If we moved away from the entrance, the Malignants might go after the soldiers and not notice us.

Fawke nodded.

We moved like ghosts, barely breathing, watching every placement of our feet. We couldn't see the outside from the interior room, and I prayed my plan would work. I stood to one side of the door, Fawke the other.

Two Malignants drifted down the stairs, hovering in the exit door. They sniffed the air before moving outside. Seconds later, gunfire erupted.

The army will never suspect we'd hidden in the same building as those things. I closed my eyes and let out the breath I'd been holding. We'd wait for the all clear.

"Lars? Roland? What's going on?" I asked after several long minutes.

"The soldiers seem to be taking a lunch break. The other men went on ahead. Guess the soldiers don't want to share. The jeep behind you has turned around and left." Roland laughed. "Looks like you're stuck for a while."

"How many out front?"

"Three."

I glanced at Fawke and raised my eyebrows. "We can take them. We'd have a jeep and that gun."

"My thoughts exactly." He grinned. "Rory, how good of an actor are you? Can you act scared? Like you need help?"

"Act?" She rolled her eyes. "I can't hardly breathe for fear."

"I'd like you to go out the back, then dash around the front, pleading for help. Keep them distracted until we get behind them. Can you do that? It'll make you a criminal same as us. You'll be hunted."

"Sure. You guys saved my life. I'll do anything you ask. There's nothing in Soriah for me." She got to her feet and squared her shoulders. "Don't let them shoot me." She whirled and raced out the back. Seconds later, she stopped a few feet from the soldiers, her hands in the air. "Please, help me. I've been attacked."

Only one of them made it to his weapon before we stepped out. "Drop it," Ezra said. "Hands up. We're going to take that gun and this jeep."

The soldiers' eyes widened. The one with the gun set it slowly on the ground. "What are you going to do to us?"

"That's up to you." Fawke picked up the gun and handed it to Dante, then patted the soldiers down. "They're clean."

I stepped forward. "My suggestion to you is that you hand over your radios and move into that building. Doing so will prevent us from shooting you."

"What if more of those things come?" The youngest soldier asked. "You're leaving us to die."

"You'd have shot us without a second thought." I tilted my head.

"We have orders to shoot." He acted as if that made a difference.

"Well, since I'm the leader of this group, I'm making the decisions now and giving the orders." I stared at him, wishing I could convince the three of them to join our side. We needed more fighters. Knowing it would take too long for them to earn my trust after Jobe's stunt, I again ordered them into the building.

"Anyone know how to drive?" I asked.

"I can figure it out," Ezra said. "Or you can force one of them to drive us."

"We'd give away the location of the compound." I shook my head. "You'll figure it out."

"We're wasting time." Fawke hopped up behind the big gun. "Let's go."

With a lot of lurching and gear grinding, Ezra drove us away from the soldiers who watched from the open doorway of the building. He stuck his arm out the jeep and made an obscene gesture. "Good luck, boys!"

I glanced at the jeep console and grinned. Three walkie-talkies. Mission one accomplished.

Mission two: Find the army base.

8

"Go to the east end," Lars said. "Eb will let you in."

We didn't have a door on that end. I glanced at Fawke who shrugged.

When we rounded the corner, an entire portion of the wall lowered, providing us a ramp to drive the jeep up and into a cavernous room. I grinned. The old man's father truly had thought of everything, and a new surprise greeted us every day.

I patted Ezra on the shoulder as I hopped down. "You need practice driving, my friend. I think I have whip lash."

"Very funny." He laughed and turned off the jeep. "I did alright."

The others gathered round as the ramp raised to close us back in. I held up a walkie-talkie. "Roland is going home."

Cheers rose. It wasn't about the boy's safety, although that was important, it was about communication with Jenkins and the others. The ability to get help when we needed.

I put Rory in Gage's capable hands and headed to the showers. Eb insisted on rationing the water, but agreed that being covered in Malignant blood warranted a hot one.

Ignoring conservation, I stepped under the hot spray and lifted my face to the water, letting it wash away not only the stench, but the cares of the day. We'd accomplished our mission. We hadn't gained any seasoned fighters, but that day would come.

I lathered my hair and body, rinsed, and then stepped reluctantly from the shower and changed into worn, but clean, army green scrubs. I glanced at the mess of rags I usually wore, suddenly missing them. I'd worn them for so long, they'd become like a second skin. My armor. I felt safe in them, exposed in the scrubs.

"Don't worry." Riva scooped them up. "I'll get them cleaned and as ugly as they were before."

"Thank you." I tied my hair into a messy bun and headed for the control room.

Roland glanced up, sadness in his eyes. "Do I have to go?"

"Yes, I promised Jenkins. The journey will be dangerous, but you making it back with the walkie talkie is a must. You'll have to run and not stop until you reach the safety of the trees. Then, find the others and have Jenkins make contact. Can you do this? It's very important."

He nodded. "Yes. Can I come back?"

I laughed, ruffling his hair. "Your day to fight will come sooner than you think. Keep training so you'll be ready." Unfortunately, we'd need every person old enough to hold a gun to help fight the upcoming war with Soriah. "We leave in the morning."

Leaving the boy with his last day of watching the monitors, I headed to the dining room where Kira had a meal waiting for me. "Rat and potatoes, your favorite."

"Gee, thanks." I'd gotten used to not thinking about the meat in front of me. Food was food.

Fawke sat across from me. "A good day."

I nodded. "If we can get soldiers in small groups like today, we can take their supplies and build our resources."

"I don't think it will always be that easy. The three we let go will rejoin their troops, re-arm themselves, and be ready to fight us again. They won't let down their guard so easily next time."

"Still thinking about sneaking in once we find their base?" My hand holding a fork paused halfway to my mouth.

He nodded. "Unless we get lucky again, yes."

"We need more people." I sounded like a broken record. "Getting soldiers to join us won't be easy. It'll take time to trust them. We can't take fighters from Rebel City unless absolutely necessary, not to mention it will take them a few days to get here."

His gaze locked on mine. "You've changed since leaving Soriah. Grown hard. While I don't like this idea any better than you do, we may have to give anyone we come across a choice. Join us or die."

"Kill them." My heart sank. I only acted hard as steel, but was nowhere close.

"Yes. We can't let the opposing army stay strong. The jail we have isn't big enough to hold even half an army." He exhaled heavily, dropping his fork beside his plate. "It'll take time to make sure we can trust them if they do come with us. I think that's why Jenkins makes newcomers fight."

"Absolutely not. I will not have anyone fight to the death."

He crossed his arms and leaned back in his chair. "We'll do the opposite, Crynn. Let them think they have to fight to the death. We only keep those not willing to outright kill."

I scrunched my lips. His idea held merit. We wanted fighters, but not murderers. People who would kill the opposition, but not relish in it. "It'll still be hard."

"We can't do this alone."

"I know." I tossed my fork on the table and stood, not liking the responsibility on my shoulders. "You make the decision."

"No, we agreed we would both lead this group, then run the idea past the others. We haven't gotten to that point yet."

"Call the rest. We'll discuss it with them." I sat and resumed eating, the food tasteless.

"You can't pick and choose when to lead, Crynn." Fawke marched to the wall and spoke into the intercom. "Everyone gather in the dining room in five minutes."

He spoke the truth. Either I led or I didn't. Either I made tough choices or let someone else take the role nobody else wanted.

The others trickled in taking their seats and focusing their attention on us. Fawke stood in the center of the room and laid out his idea.

Impassive faces stared at us. When no one spoke, I got to my feet. "Ezra, you've killed before. That's why you're in this god forsaken place. What do you think of this idea? Could you kill someone in a fight like Jenkins had me participate in?"

He rolled his shoulders. "No. I killed a man in self-defense. He just happened to be a palace guard."

"Samson?" I turned to the big man next to him, his eyes wide in his dark face.

"Only when backed into a corner."

"So, if they refuse to join us," Kira asked, "we'll execute them? That makes us no better than those making the rules in Soriah. I'm opposed to the idea."

"If they are willing to fight," Jolt said, "release them outside. Sure, they might make it back to the army, but let the Supreme Being decide their fate. We aren't God." His gaze flickered to the pretty Rory.

"Well said." I smiled and resumed my seat. "We can do a round of questions, then test if they'll fight. If not, how else can we gain their trust? I don't want a repeat of Jobe."

"We've got time," Fawke said. "I need volunteers to go with me and Crynn tomorrow to escort Roland to the edge of the city."

Moses, Dante, and the twins, Ted and Ned volunteered.

"That's enough," I said. "A smaller group has a better chance of not getting noticed.

"Incoming," Lars said through the intercom. "Two men, one woman. Look like scouts."

"We'll keep the rest of you updated on the tests," I said, before heading to the control room, Fawke at my side.

Those outside looked like scouts only because they weren't wearing a uniform. A group of Malignants stepped from the shadows. The woman screamed and raced for the Ferris Wheel.

"That's the largest group of monsters I've seen in days," Lars said.

"And those people brought them right to us." I shook my head. "There's too many for us to fight. We'd need everyone out there. We can't take that risk."

"They're climbing the wheel." Fawke pointed to a different monitor. "They'll have to hold on until the Malignants leave."

"They won't leave as long as food is in sight." I paced the room. "We need to draw them away." I headed for the door.

Fawke grabbed my arm. "It's suicide to go out there."

"I'm looking for Eb." I frowned, pulling free. "He might have an idea."

"Sorry." He followed me to Eb's room.

The old habit of the leader being his assignment, keep alive at all costs, hadn't stopped. It bothered me then, and bothered me now.

I knocked and entered when told to. Eb sat at a small table, papers spread in front of him. "What's happening?"

I told him of our need to draw the Malignants away. "I'm sure the people out there have no idea we're here, but they'll die without help."

"There's the siren and some flares. Both would draw the attention of the army." He rubbed his whiskered chin. "You could take the jeep out. Draw them away. Someone else can let the strangers in and put them in the cell until you return."

Fawke shook his head. "We'd attract too much attention by speeding through a debris filled city. We'd have to lose them and circle back. We might lead the army right to us."

"We can't get Roland safely away with a group that size outside." I crossed my arms.

"Then I say take a couple of people, slip out the back and run like the devil is on your heels, because he is." Eb motioned to the papers in front of him. "Not to change the subject, but I've been studying maps of the city. There's an area that used to be quite a substantial park to the north. From the looks of it here, it's large enough to house an army."

"Fine. Back to the task at hand, please." I glanced at Fawke. "I'll be the decoy."

"Absolutely not." A muscle ticked in his jaw. "Use the intercom to tell those people to go around back. If they're fast, they'll make it. We'll let them in that way. Not one of us will set foot outside until those things leave."

I opened my mouth to argue, then clamped it shut. We'd do it his way and hope for the best.

Back in the control room, I pulled the microphone to me. "You out there."

The three outside glanced around from their perch in a dangling car on the now dead ride.

"We can offer you sanctuary, but you need to get to the side door on the east side of this building. You won't have much time. Those things will be on you in a heartbeat. Raise your hand if you understand."

All three raised their hands.

"Do not make a move until I say." I stepped back. "Now what?"

"I'll bang on the front door." Fawke shrugged. "It might mean we can't leave in the morning. It'll take days for those things to go away. When you see them leave the area under the wheel, give the order to run."

I nodded and turned back to those hovering above a hungry horde.

Several minutes later, the Malignants turned and left. Since the wheel was right above us, they wouldn't be far away. Those three people needed to move faster than they ever had.

"Go. Look for an open door. Now!"

They scurried like rats, one of the men helping the woman. Once on the ground, the Malignants shrieked and darted toward them.

I raced for the east door, opening it just enough to see them coming. "Make it fast. I won't take a chance for those things getting in."

They dove inside, landing in a heap on the concrete floor.

I slammed the door.

The monsters banged against it.

"If you hadn't of opened that door, we'd never have seen it. You're well hidden here." One of the men peered up at me from the floor.

"That's the idea." I motioned for Dante to take their weapons. "I apologize for the fact that we'll need to lock you up."

"Beats getting eaten by those things." He helped the woman to her feet and grinned. "Jenkins sent us. The city has had a bit of trouble."

9

"What kind of trouble?" Ice trickled down my spine, taking root in my stomach.

"The complex at the top of the mountain is unlivable. He sent us to tell you to expect them here, in this city, in a week's time."

I widened my eyes. "They're coming here?"

The man shrugged. "He's hoping you'll meet them since they have no idea whether you made it to this place. Our goal was to find you…if we could. Jenkins doesn't remember where this place is, only that it's here and that there was a giant wheel rising into the sky. That was our beacon. I'm Jerome, this is Hanford, and this is Ella. He sent us because we have no family. We're expendable."

They weren't expected to survive. No one was expendable, despite what Soriah thought.

I sagged against the wall. Jenkins was leading a community of around a hundred people, mostly women and children, through a monster infested city, with an army looking for them, to a place he can't remember the exact location of. All in hopes that we'll find them. The man's desperation spurred me to make a quick decision.

"How will they come?"

"Sticking as much to the tree line as possible, then staying outside the city to the west."

"Why not stay somewhere else on the mountain?"

The man sighed. "The monsters have arrived there. There's been evidence of deer being killed. Bird carcasses. Since there's little left of them, it's easy to figure out how the animals died."

Eb rapped his cane. "Enough talking. There's work to be done. How long did it take you to get here?"

"Three days."

"That gives us four to meet them, two days at the most to prepare. Crynn, Fawke, follow me. Kira, take care of our guests. They've earned a good meal." He turned and headed to his room, me and Fawke following.

"Space is not an issue," he said, closing the door behind us. "Food is. We'll set more rat traps and plant more crops. The big issue is finding those people before those things or the army does. It'll be hard to keep children quiet. Especially if they're frightened. Time and strength is of the essence."

I nodded. "I'll leave Roland and Rory with you to help you until we get back." If we made it back. "I need every available fighter to keep that group safe. We'll need your eyes the best you can give them."

"Understood." His face fell. "Let's pray you make it back safely. In the meantime, I'll prepare the best I can. I expect you to be gone at least a day. Once you move further than three blocks in any direction, I'll have no cameras to watch you on."

I nodded again. "We need to go prepare. We'll leave a few weapons behind, but that armory might just be what saves our lives."

Fawke and I headed to the secret room in the control room. I explained to Lars and Roland the new plan. "Roland, Eb will need you while we're gone."

"I'll do whatever I need to." Worry flickered in his dark eyes. "Just keep the community safe."

"We'll do our best." I smiled and pressed the button to open the panel. One-by-one, I lay flame throwers, grenades, ammunition, and guns on the floor. We'd have the firepower, but if we ran across the army, we'd still be outnumbered. "We're going to need the gun on the jeep."

"I'll have Ezra fill the gas tank and make sure the machine gun has plenty of ammo. We'll only fire if absolutely necessary," Fawke said.

It'd be necessary. Once the Malignants got wind of such a large group of humans, they'd come in droves. If we had to fire, hopefully the army would think it some of their own doing the shooting. A whole lot of hope and ifs. God be with us.

The next two days were spent making plans. When we left, Ezra would drive. Dante would man the machine gun. The rest of us, heavily armed, would walk alongside the jeep, taking the road outside of the city to intercept Jenkins and the others.

Kira packed our backpacks with as much food and water as we could each carry, except for hers. Her pack held medical supplies. "This is insane. What is Jenkins thinking?"

"He's trying to keep his people safe." Jerome said.

I'd have done the same. Sometimes flight is the only way. "Get some rest. We leave early."

I slept little that night wondering if we'd prepared enough. Made enough plans to keep us all alive. Praying we didn't run across the army or so many Malignants we couldn't fight them off. I woke the next morning with gritty eyes and the beginning of a headache.

After washing my face, I headed to the dining room for a quick breakfast of stale bread smeared with something I didn't recognize. I scarfed it down and joined Fawke and the others at the jeep.

Eb supervised the loading of the ammunition. "I've checked the oil and the tires. That's the extent of my mechanical know how." He faced me. "I'll do everything I can to let you know when danger is coming."

"I appreciate it." I held out my hand. "We'll be back."

"Sure." His smile looked forced. "I hope so. I've gotten use to the company."

I glanced to where Jolt gave Rory a quick kiss and smiled. He'd do everything he could to get back to her if the look on their faces was any indication of how they were starting to feel about each other.

I smiled at Fawke.

"Someday, this will end." He took my hand. "We'll build a new life without the tyranny of Soriah or the threat of Malignants."

I held onto his words. A peaceful life was all I'd ever wanted. Feeling older than my years, I told everyone it was time to go. I didn't worry about them out there. Except for the three Jenkins had sent, we weren't facing anything we hadn't faced before and bored the physical and emotional scars to prove it.

Eb opened the big door and Ezra drove the jeep out. The rest of us followed, quickly disposing of the few Malignants milling about. The larger group of them still gathered around the Ferris wheel as if their lost meal would suddenly reappear.

We headed away from them, skirting around the park and through a small section of the city until all we saw was fields of dry grass. Nothing stirred. No breeze blew. Unless spotted, the Malignants wouldn't be able to know we were there. I wasn't such a fool as to think our luck would last, but I'd take it for as long as possible.

The jeeps wheels rumbled over cracked pavement, crushing smaller rocks and cement blocks under its tires. Our footsteps made no sound over the noise of the vehicle.

I let Jerome lead, taking us the way they'd come. My heart skipped a beat at every shriek coming from the city.

Fawke put a reassuring hand on my shoulder. "We'll be fine."

"What about those we're going to meet? How many of them will have survived this nightmarish trek? If they came across the—"

"Don't invite worry, Crynn." He gave my shoulder a gentle squeeze. "We'll do what we can for whoever is left. Jenkins isn't an idiot. He'll have done everything in his power to protect his people. Why else make such a trip?"

True. I focused my attention on the buildings to my right, switching occasionally to the fields on my left. I didn't expect trouble to come from there. Malignants preferred the safety of the buildings. Not the wide open spaces.

Gunfire erupted from far off, then ceased. A few minutes later, it started again. The army, unknowingly, cleared the area of monsters to make our travel easier. We killed a few straggling beasts with our swords and continued marching toward the mountain.

Screams erupted from up ahead, spurring us faster. Malignants sprinted toward Jenkins' group. The men, swords drawn, circled the women and children. One man raised his sword with a yell and bolted forward, only to disappear under the four monsters who overtook him.

We were too close to shoot. We might hit an innocent. I unsheathed my sword and raced to the fight, my people right alongside me.

I whirled, slashed, jabbed like a dervish, keeping myself between the monsters and the civilians. The rotten stench of Malignant blood covered me, making my hands slippery. Still, I fought on, felling one demon after another until I lost count.

Those with Jenkins that could fight joined us. Several fell. One woman dropped her child as a Malignant leapt on her back.

Fawke snatched the child from the ground, tossing it to another woman as if it weighed nothing. This time, instead of fighting by my side, he fought to protect the children.

Ezra and Dante flanked me. The others did their

best to keep their backs to those unable to fight.

By the time more than twenty Malignants lay dead at our feet, only two humans had died. The mother and the man who had charged. Several more were wounded. No one bit, thankfully.

"We rest," I ordered. "If you're injured, see Kira." I leaned heavily on my sword, my breathing coming in gasps.

"Thank you for coming." Jenkins, blood streaking his face, stepped to my side. "We wouldn't have made it without your warriors."

"We can't rest long. More will come. We have half a day of fast walking to reach the compound. It's safer to travel at night, but from the exhaustion on the children's faces, they need a bed, not a field to sleep in." I glanced around his group. "There aren't as many of you as I thought there would be."

He shook his head, sadness clouding his features. "We've lost a lot. Some before leaving the mountain. The Malignants found a new source of food."

Gunfire erupted in the distance again.

He laughed without humor. "Never thought I'd be happy to have the army so close."

"Me either." I turned and accepted the canteen of water Riva handed me. "Kira? Can the injured move?"

"They have no choice. They can walk. That's enough. I've put the more serious wounded in the jeep."

I ordered everyone to their feet. "We make haste. The smaller ones will have to be carried. No talking. No crying. One foot in front of the other. This is not an easy hike."

I glanced at Jenkins to see how well he accepted me taking charge. I tilted my head.

He nodded. "I have come to your territory, Crynn. You're the leader of these people now. I have no experience out here."

"Good." I didn't need his interference in my plans to bring down first the army, then Soriah.

10

Another group of Malignants stalked us, hanging back. I moved to the end of the line of people where Fawke marched.

"Are they afraid of the jeep?" I asked.

"Maybe. If they've witnessed the army mowing down others of them, they might be more cautious at the sight of that big gun."

When I noticed the group slowing, curious as to what Fawke and I were doing, I ordered them on. The Malignants were only biding their time and growing in numbers.

"We'll be overrun." My heart threatened to beat free. My palms sweat around the hilt of my blade.

"Go get the flame thrower. If they get close enough, use it. If that doesn't slow them down, we'll have to open fire and risk alerting the army."

I nodded and dashed for the jeep, returning a few minutes later with the flame thrower balanced on my shoulder. I'd never be able to aim it correctly. The weight was too much for me.

Fawke took it. "Move these people faster."

I nodded and marched up and down the line, urging them on, encouraging them with promises of beds and food. Silent tears ran down the pale faces of several of the children, their mothers quietly pleading with them to not make a sound.

"These people can't go on without a rest." Jenkins fell into step beside me. "The mothers and fathers are carrying the little ones. It slows them down."

"Where do you suggest we stop?" I narrowed my eyes. "Have you seen the horde following us? They'll do so all the way to the compound. We'll be locked in for days." Better locked in than dead. "If we do find an empty building big enough, they'll surround the place. It's best if we keep on, not stopping until we reach the compound."

"There you are." Lars spoke into my ear. "Quite the group, and I'm not talking about the humans."

"Good to hear your voice. Any advice on how to get away from them?"

"No, and it's starting to look like rain. You've got to hurry."

I glanced at the swirling dark clouds overhead. "We need a place to wait it out." My stomach dropped.

"There isn't anywhere close to house that many. Maybe run?"

Easy for him to say. I glanced at Jenkins. "We need to make it back before it rains." Hopefully, fear would put wings on the feet of the people. "You have no trees here to filter out the poison."

He blanched and nodded. "Okay, people. We have to run. I know you're tired, but it's going to rain and we've got followers approaching."

I ordered Ezra to hold the jeep back and called my fighters to join me. We'd have to cover the fleeing crowd. Once they ran, the Malignants would give chase. "Jerome, lead the people to the compound. At the back, a large door will open big enough for everyone to get inside. Don't stop. Get them there no matter what. If someone falls, the others keep going. We'll cover you."

I pulled the strap holding my rifle over my shoulder and took aim. "Dante, open fire as soon as the horde is close enough." We'd have to take our chances with the army.

"Are there any Malignants between us and the compound?" I asked.

"No," Roland replied. "But more are coming to join that group. You'd better get out of there."

We moved slowly backward as Jenkins' people broke into a run. The horde following shrieked and sprinted toward us.

Fawke opened fire with the flame thrower, filling the air with the stench of burning flesh.

Bile rose in my throat.

Dante fired the machine gun, mowing down the second line of offense.

Then, those of us with rifles, started shooting.

"When they're close, switch to swords. We can't risk shooting each other." I continued to shoot, the machine gun rattling over my head. "Fighting circle!"

"Army coming," Lars said. "Small group headed your way."

Good. They'd help us fight. We'd worry about

them afterward…if we stayed alive.

Ten men in military uniform burst from an alley and joined the fray, aiming pistols at the monster's heads and dropping them like flies as they made their way to our circle.

"Sergeant Larsen at your service," one of them said. "You're under arrest for treason." He shot a monster as it opened its mouth to shriek.

"Seriously?" I swung, decapitating one. "We'll discuss this later. Talk to me, guys." I spoke into my earpiece.

"No more coming. If you can dispose of that group, you'll be clear. The rebel group is one block from the compound," Lars said. "Good luck with the jerk sergeant."

I chuckled despite the danger in front of me.

One of the beasts broke through our ranks, launching itself at Larsen. The soldier screamed, using both hands to hold the creature's snapping teeth away from his neck.

I lunged forward, driving my sword through its back and into its heart stopping just short of impaling the soldier. "You're welcome." Instead of helping him to his feet, I rejoined the fight until the remaining Malignants fled.

Two soldiers lay dead, along with one of ours. I stood over the slashed body of Jep, one of the criminals sent to us before we'd found the mountain refuge.

"All clear," Roland said. "Rebels are safe inside. Time for you to come home."

"I've got some business to tend to first." I aimed my gun at the sergeant's heart.

Immediately, the remaining eight soldiers aimed at me, only to have my fighters train their weapons on them. I grinned. "Stalemate."

"You'll die, Miss Dayholt."

"I'm not afraid of dying, Sergeant. Can you say the same? You screamed like a little girl when that thing tackled you."

"Let's start over." He held out his hand. "Sergeant Larsen, deserter from the Army of Soriah. I only joked about the arrest. Tried to lighten the mood."

"How do I know you're telling the truth?"

He shrugged. "You don't."

"Why did you desert?" Fawke asked.

"Because the army ordered us to assassinate two Stalkers who recently landed. We couldn't." He glanced at his group. "We took them into the city and told them to hide when we saw the horde heading your way."

"Where are they now and why kill Stalkers?"

He put two fingers to his lips and gave a shrill whistle. "No idea why our commander wanted them dead. They're supposed to be on our side."

Two young men ventured from the nearest building. They could be soldiers in disguise, but the fear on their faces gave me the impression they were who Larsen said they were.

"When did you drop?"

"A few days ago," one said. "A girl was with us, but she didn't drop in the same place. The wind took her out of sight."

"Her name?" Three new Stalkers at once? Had Soriah rigged the Wheel to land on black more often?

I wouldn't put it past them.

"Rory."

I nodded. "She's safe with us. Excuse me." I motioned for Fawke to step away with me from the others.

"What do you think?"

"They could have shot us once the Malignants were disposed of."

"Yes, but we outnumber them."

"You're the one Soriah wants dead. The target is bigger on your back."

"Get rid of you, Miss Dayholt," Larsen said, "and they hope the others will turn themselves in."

That would never happen. My friends would continue the fight.

I turned back to the new Stalkers. "Do you have a radio?"

They nodded.

"Good." I wanted to have a conversation with Sharon.

"Huh," Roland cleared his throat. "You have a problem."

"What?"

"Two jeeps heading your way. One block to the east."

"Let's move." I turned and raced for the Ferris wheel rising in the distance.

Since the eight soldiers kept pace with us, rather than detain us, I guessed they were honest about being deserters. I'd consult with Fawke, but didn't see a need to grill them with questions. Running with us seemed proof enough we could trust them.

"Turn right through that building," Lars said.

"You'll come out into an alley."

"The jeep can't do that," Ezra said.

"Sorry. You'll have to meet up just past the building."

"Everyone stays together," I said. "We follow the jeep." The vehicle was too valuable to lose.

The jeep careened around the corner of a four-story building, then left down an alley. From a block over I heard the roar of another jeep's engine.

"Do you think they know we're here?" I asked.

Larsen shook his head. "They'll find the dead Malignants and my two soldiers. They'll think the rest of us either dead or trying to find our way back to the camp. The only fly in the ointment will be your dead that were left behind."

"We need to remove your tracking devices." I pulled my knife, Fawke doing the same. "You can't come with us otherwise."

He held out his arm.

Once the devices were cut from their skin, we ground them under our boots and continued our wild sprint around another building, finally stepping onto the cracked pavement of the long dead amusement park. I wanted to blindfold the soldiers, but knew we couldn't stop long enough. Stopping would allow the army to catch up with us. I had no choice but to trust them.

Instead, I led the way to the back door and waited while Eb lowered it. "Hurry. We can't let them know this place exists."

Larsen waved his soldiers forward. The rest of us followed and the door raised.

"Welcome to your new home, ladies and

gentlemen." I stared at the wide-eyed faces of the rebel community. "You'll have rooms, food, water, all your needs will be met. You cannot go outside. This underground complex is your new home. At least for now. Welcome to the new Rebel City."

Despite their exhaustion, jubilant yells echoed in the cavernous room.

Tears shimmered in the eyes of the usually tough Jenkins. "I remember this place."

"As I remember the young you." Eb stepped into the room.

"Mr. Ebenezer." Jenkins rushed forward and wrapped the old man in a hug. "You're still here."

"The only one until these people came." He smiled. "Come. We can catch up later. You must all be tired and hungry. Crynn, you're needed in the control room." His smile faded as his gaze landed on the soldiers. "Sergeant, you might as well accompany her."

I raised my eyebrows, but headed to the control room with Fawke and Larsen. "What's going on?"

"The army has stopped at the edge of the park." Lars pointed at the screen.

"What are they doing, Sergeant?" I motioned him over.

"Surveying the area. You people have done well. There's no sign of life here. They'll move on."

"Are you sure?"

"Pretty sure. Our task here was to find the rebels, you in particular, and to get rid of as many of those things as we can. Soriah wants this place back. The white city is getting overpopulated."

So, the reason for Stalkers wasn't a complete lie.

They did want the Malignants gone. But that still didn't explain why the army commander wanted the new Stalkers dead. "I don't think Soriah realizes how many of the Malignants there are. Not to mention the fact they breed."

"That's new information." His brows rose.

"Imagine our surprise when we found the nests," Fawke said. "We intend to sneak into the army camp and do our best to disable them. We're going to need your help."

"You'll have it, but I think it wise to let them rid the city of monsters, at least as much as possible. The army has a purpose right now. If this place is as safe as you say, they won't find us here."

"Unless they start digging," Eb said, "they won't find us. Especially after all this time. There has to be several feet of dust on top of this place. The doors cannot be detected from the outside. Unless someone lets them know we're here, we're safe. Radios, please. On the table."

Larsen removed his radio from his belt. "I'll collect the others."

"Now, please."

"Yes, sir."

I laughed as he left. "Used to following orders, that one."

"Don't let down your guard just yet. That army will be looking for their soldiers. Until they find bodies, they'll believe them to be alive."

I nodded. "We'll follow Larsen's advice and let the army do the dirty work for us. That gives us time to figure out a way to get into their camp undetected."

11

After cleaning up and changing to clothes not covered in blood, I leaned heavily on the sink. My hands gripped the cold porcelain as I stared into the mirror not recognizing the person I'd become.

I'd left behind our dead. I'd ordered civilians to be left if they couldn't keep up. Who was the monster here? I was no better than President Cane. I took a deep shuddering breath and pushed away from the sink.

Outside the showers, Fawke lounged against the wall, leg bent, foot planted against the concrete blocks that made up the walls. "You alright?"

Nodding, I stopped in front of him. "Doing some soul searching."

His right hand cupped my cheek. "Did it do any good?" His gaze softened, his words barely above a whisper.

"No." I leaned into his touch. "Why haven't you kissed me yet?" Did he not want me? Had he discovered the monster inside me?

He dropped his hand and straightened. "Romance

complicates things. I can't let my heart get any deeper into…us. Not until this is over. One of us might not make it through."

"What if it never ends?"

He exhaled heavily. "Then I'll do some soul searching of my own."

I breathed deeply through my nose and stepped back. "Let's meet with Larsen. He's our greatest asset right now."

"You trust him?"

"We don't have a choice." I turned and marched to the dining room, stopping by the control room first. "Army still out there?"

Lars nodded. "A few are on foot wandering around the park looking for signs they'll never find."

"This place is well concealed." Even the large door blended in with the landscape. "Keep me posted. When is Dayton on watch?"

"In another hour. Roland has gone to spend some time with his family."

Good. The boy deserved it.

"Crynn?" Kira rushed into the room. "We have a problem."

I turned. "What?"

"One of the injured civilians was bit. He didn't seem severe so I checked him out last."

My blood ran cold. My gaze met Fawke's serious one. "I'm coming."

We followed her to the infirmary where a man lay shackled to the bed.

"He'll turn," she said.

"Can we wait and see the transformation?" Fawke asked. "Maybe study him? We know so little about those things."

"We don't know for sure that a bite means he'll turn, but it's always been suspected." Kira leaned over him. "I've cleaned his wound the best I could, cutting away the flesh already dying. I suppose we can wait and see."

"How long?" I stared at the seeping bandage around his arm.

"I have no idea." Kira covered him up. "My medical knowledge barely prevents normal infections. It's not exactly a sterile world out there."

"The army has a full medical tent," Larsen said from behind us. "There is medicine that will supposedly help against bites, although no one knows for sure. We need those supplies."

I turned. "You're going to help us get them. Follow me." I led the way to the dining room and a large empty table, asking Gage to find some paper. "We'll need a map of the camp and the easiest way to get there. Can you draw one?"

He nodded. "I've been here since the army arrived. I know that place like the lines on my hand."

I barely glanced up as the Gage brought the paper and a pencil. Someone else placed bowls of soup in front of us. I didn't know if we could infiltrate the camp in time to help the bitten man, but we'd do our best.

Larsen drew a large compound marking where the jeeps were kept, the armory, the infirmary, the commander's tent, and the tents housing the soldiers. "It won't be easy with close to three hundred soldiers, but guards are at a minimum from midnight to three a.m. since the Malignants rarely venture out after dark."

"Then that's when we'll go." I sat and took a bite of my meal. "Hey, this isn't rat."

Soran smiled. "The new group brought venison. It won't last long, but it's something different for today."

For that I was thankful, spooning a slice of carrot to my mouth. "When do we go?"

"As soon as we're ready," Fawke said, digging into his own bowl. "We'll need a small group. Easier to sneak in undetected."

"We'll take Ezra, Dante, Gage, and Moses. Kira is needed here. Sergeant, we'll need you. The other soldiers will remain behind." Six of our original seven. The people I trusted the most to watch my back. "Is tomorrow night too late? We need to rest."

Fawke shrugged. "No one knows how long it takes a bite to finish a person. But, I agree. We need to rest after the day we've had. We'll have to take the chance."

Wonderful. Bet on the poor man's life. Unfortunately, we'd be no good to anyone exhausted. I shoved my empty bowl away. "I'm headed to bed. Goodnight."

I didn't bother changing from the scrubs I wore and lay on my back staring at the ceiling, cursing the wheel that had sent me here. Fate had made me leader. A role no one else wanted to take from me. A role I'd willingly give up.

The next morning, I shrugged off the self-pity and prepared to face another long day. I made my first stop the control room, where Dayton said the soldiers had moved on shortly before nightfall.

"Call Moses and Ezra to prepare the weapons we'd need tonight, please." I patted his shoulder and headed to breakfast where Fawke Larsen already sat poring over the map the sergeant had drawn.

Fawke tapped the paper. "We figure we'll go in here. The grass is high, and the tents close together. We'll have room to hide."

"Those are the barracks." Larsen nodded. "Everyone except the two guards patrolling the perimeter will be asleep."

"The army doesn't expect anyone to be foolish enough to come," I said.

"Crynn to the control room." Dayton's voice sounded loud over the intercom. "Radio is trying to come on. There isn't good reception here."

Sharon.

I raced down the hall, telling Larsen to stay behind. The last thing we needed was for her to see him and know we had army deserters.

I skidded to a halt as the monitor came to life. "Hello." I grinned, meeting the woman's startled gaze.

"Don't tell me you have my new Stalkers." Her eyes hardened.

"Yep."

"Where are you? What is that place?"

"Our new home." I waved an arm. "Welcome to Rebel City."

"Even with the new three, you are no match for us, Miss Dayholt."

"We'll see about that." I crossed my arms. "May I pass on your message?"

"There is no message. I simply had the need to

make sure they landed safely since they didn't contact me as ordered."

So, she hadn't planned on them being killed. Why had the commander made that decision?

"I'll let them know of your concern." I kept my smile in place.

"Exactly what are your plans, Miss Dayholt? Surely, you realize you cannot win this fight."

I leaned closer to the monitor. "We'll see about that. I'd watch your back if I were you. Something you might want to pass onto President Cane. Signing off." I pressed the button, flickering the screen off as she pressed her lips in a straight line.

I glanced up to see Fawke and Larsen in the doorway. "Why does your commander want Stalkers dead?"

"Because he knows that given the chance, they'll join you," Larsen said. "Why would young people with no fighting skills want to stay out there? With you, they learn to fight, thus becoming the enemy. I doubt Soriah will send any more."

I agreed. Either they'd remove the black square on the wheel or have it stand for something else. We'd get no more fighters that way.

"Increase training of all men and women sixteen and older, unless they're a mother. We're going to need as many soldiers of our own as we can get in order to fight Soriah." I passed them and stepped into the hall, calling over my shoulder for Dayton to call all that meet those requirements to the training hall.

"Has anyone seen Eb?" I asked.

"Last I heard, he was in the garden." Dayton pressed buttons on his keypad. "Yep. He's supervising the planting of more crops."

"I'll meet you two in the training room," I told Fawke and Larsen. "I want to talk to Eb."

I headed to the garden where Eb sat on a crate, telling several teenagers how to plant the seeds. "We're going to the army camp tonight."

"Ah."

"One of the newcomers was bitten."

He glanced up, startled. "What does that mean?"

"We aren't exactly sure. Kira is watching over him. If he turns, I need you to give the order to have him put down."

"Why me?" Leaning on his cane, he pushed to his feet.

"This was your home first. With me gone, you're the boss."

"Give that job to Jenkins. I don't want it."

I put my hand on his arm. "You're the wisest person we have. I'm relying on your experience to keep these people safe."

"Fine. I'll assess the situation and make the decision as I see fit."

That would have to do. "I'll tell Jenkins not to make any decisions until he speaks with you." Between the two of them, the people here would remain safe.

"You're making preparations in case you don't return."

"Yes. There is always that possibility."

"Go with God, Crynn."

I found Jenkins headed to the training room. I filled him in on my discussion with Eb. "Can you work with him?"

"Of course. Don't worry. We'll be fine here. You concentrate on getting back with your group. We'll keep an eye on the wounded man."

Confident I'd done all that I could, I joined the others in the training room. I dismissed the few elderly and the mothers. The others I lined up, assessing their ability to fight. I grinned at the sight of Roland, head high, shoulders back.

"You are not sixteen, young man."

"I can fight." His eyes flashed.

"You are needed more here. I feel safer with your eyes on the monitor. Be my eyes, Roland."

He huffed and stepped out of line.

Another young man kept his gaze averted.

"I seriously think you, too, are underage."

"No, ma'am."

"Is your mother here?" I arched a brow. "I'd like to ask her."

He groaned and stepped out of line.

A young woman with one leg shorter than the other got dismissed, along with a woman noticeably pregnant.

"I appreciate everyone's willingness to fight for our freedom," I said, marching up and down the line. "But able bodies are also needed here. If you want to train, you are free to do so, but when the fight comes, only those I choose will go. The others will stay to defend this place." Hopefully, that would make them feel valued.

"The coming war will be a dangerous one. Many will perish. I have tough choices to make and will abide by the ones I make. The soldiers will be in charge of your training. I will expect a full report each day on your progress." I glanced at Larsen who nodded. "Any questions?"

"Down with Soriah!" One man shouted.

Soon, the room echoed with the chant.

Pride filled me.

With the spirit of these people, we could win this war.

12

A few minutes after eleven p.m., we slipped out of the compound and followed Larsen through the city. We made little sound, skirting around obstacles like ghosts.

My nerves tingled the farther we got from safety. My mind whirled with the possibility the sergeant could be leading us into a trap.

Fawke moved closer to me, his presence calming. He always knew exactly what to do as if we shared same emotions. He reached over and gave my hand a quick squeeze.

I gave a trembling smile. We'd accomplished a lot in the few months I'd been there. Why worry that it would all end tonight? We were smart, we were brave, we were strong, we had the element of surprise on our side.

Fist high, Larsen called a halt, slipping back to join Fawke and I. "See that cluster of tents? That's the barracks. Since the commander doesn't expect anyone to be foolish enough to slip through hundreds of soldiers, it isn't patrolled. We can cut the fence and slip in there," he whispered.

I nodded, ushering the others closer in order to keep my voice low. "Take as much as you can carry. Focus on weapons and grenades. I'll head for the infirmary."

"Do not leave my side," Fawke whispered.

Ezra used bolt cutters to snap the wires making up the fence and rolled it back just enough for us to squeeze through.

My backpack snagged on the fence. I froze at the rattling, waiting for a cry of alarm.

Someone inside the nearest tent groaned.

Larsen shot me a glare over his shoulder.

After precious seconds wasted freeing my strap, I followed Larsen between two tents. He pointed across a wide pathway to a tent with a red cross painted on the side.

"There will be patients and doctors. We'll have to quietly subdue them in order to get the medical supplies. We should leave that tent for last. The armory is that darker one to the left. It will be guarded by at least one soldier," he whispered. "I'll take care of him, then go to the infirmary with you while the men raid the weapons."

I nodded, realizing his uniform will come in handy, helping him blend in without raising suspicion. If he was going to betray us, now would be the time.

With my heart in my throat, I kept my gaze locked on Larsen as he strolled toward the armory. The guard straightened and started to speak, only to have his neck broken before he could utter a word. Larsen dragged him into the tent and waved us forward.

"I'm going to the infirmary with you," Fawke said.

"You're needed at the armory." I narrowed my eyes.

"Not going to happen."

I groaned and ran toward the infirmary, Larsen and Fawke on my heels. The rest ducked into the armory. Four men to carry as many weapons as possible while Fawke shadowed me as if I were still his assignment. That had ended when we turned our backs on Soriah.

Larsen had me wait outside while he entered the infirmary. He returned a few seconds later. "One doctor on duty. The other is taking a bathroom break. We have to hurry. That gives us ten minutes max."

"Let's do this in five." I moved the tent flap aside.

The doctor had been bound and gagged. Five patients slept in curtained off alcoves. I gained a bit of respect for the sergeant seeing he hadn't killed the doctor and marched to a tall metal cabinet.

I filled my pack as full as possible, then stepped aside while Fawke did the same. In six minutes we raced from the infirmary.

Outside, I glanced around for the others in time to see them exiting back through the cut fence, their packs bulging. The mission had been too easy. A thought that made me shudder.

"Go." Fawke pushed me forward.

A shout of alarm rang out.

I glanced back to see a doctor round the corner of the tent. He shouted again, spurring us faster as soldiers poured from their tents in various modes of undress. One raised a gun and fired.

Larsen grunted and fell to his knees just as he made his way through the fence. "Leave me."

"No more left behind." I shoved my shoulder under one arm, while Fawke did the same.

By now, more soldiers had awakened and raced our way. "Dante."

He raised a flame thrower and set the closest tents on fire, temporarily blocking us from the soldiers' views. "Make haste people. This won't hold them for long."

I stumbled under the sergeant's weight. Ezra stepped back and took my place. I moved to take up the rear only to have Dante shove me forward.

"You're the leader. Lead."

Arguing would be useless. I led them through a dark building, then another, and another until the voices of the soldiers faded. They'd be coming after us with jeeps soon. We'd be surrounded.

I studied the way Larsen dragged his leg, slowing us down. No. I'd vowed not to leave anymore behind. If we were caught, so be it.

"Don't stop for me," he said. "I'll crawl if I have to. Otherwise, my head will be on a stake as an example to the troops. That's plenty of motivation to keep me moving. We have to hurry before we lead them straight to the compound."

Determination etched on Fawke's and Ezra's faces as they picked up the pace, forcing Larsen to hop, sometimes walk on his injured leg. Blood poured down his uniform. He'd be lucky if he didn't bleed out before we arrived at our destination.

I quickly unwrapped the scarf around my neck

and tied it as tightly around his leg as possible. "We run now." I raised my gaze to search his face.

"If it comes down to it, I'll finish myself off and save you the trouble," he said. "I won't risk the rest of you."

"Let's hope it doesn't come to that." I whirled and darted across the street and into another building in hopes of covering our tracks.

Shrieks came from upstairs. I'd woken sleeping monsters. We'd take our chances outside from now on.

"Head left," Lars said as soon as we stepped into the alley.

"Any sign of the army?"

"Not yet. You're three blocks from home. Pick up the pace."

I led at as fast of a pace as the men hauling Larsen could handle. We'd have to rely on protection from heaven and Lars's direction to survive the night.

The packs grew heavier with each step, yet I didn't dare slow. Rest would come with death or reaching home.

"Three jeeps one block away," Lars said through the earpiece. "You'll never make it."

"Moses, Ezra, and Dante, you three get Larsen to Kira. Fawke and I will lead the soldiers away, then circle back when it's safe." I handed my pack to Ezra.

Fawke gave his to Moses. "God speed."

"Be careful," Larsen said through gritted teeth. "This soldier isn't worth the rest of you."

"I'll determine that." I forced a smile, then sprinted for the jeeps, knowing without looking back that Fawke followed.

Once the jeeps came into sight, we darted in and out of cover, leading them away from the compound. Gunfire rattled behind us, sending chunks of concrete our way. We zig-zagged as we ran hoping to become a more difficult target.

I veered right, through a rusty gate and across a courtyard the jeeps couldn't manage. Occasionally, we'd allow them a glimpse of us, before darting out of sight again.

Breathless, I stopped, pressing my back against the crumbling wall of what had once been a fueling station. "I hope this stupid idea works."

"It allows the others to get what's important back to the compound."

I nodded. As much as I hated to admit it, Fawke and I were expendable in comparison to medical supplies and weapons. I glanced at a building towering over us. "Could we hide up there?"

"The jeeps are still following the two of you," Lars said. "If you can find a hiding place within being seen, then go for it. Otherwise, you'll be trapped."

"How far away?"

"Half a block."

Too close. No more rest. I pushed away from the wall and ran.

Bullets kicked up the dust at my feet. For the first time since arriving in the burning city, I prayed for rain as thunder rumbled overhead. Fawke and I could hide, the soldiers would have to return to their camp and the safety of their tents.

Lightening streaked across the sky, but no drops fell.

Fawke grabbed my arm and yanked me into yet another building, skidding to a halt at the sight of sleeping Malignants.

I held my breath, afraid to move, afraid to breathe. These were no ordinary Malignants. These were sleeping mothers guarding their infants.

The jeeps rumbled past.

The monsters stirred.

Fawke and I ducked into an alcove. We were goners if discovered.

I couldn't breathe. My limbs trembled. My vision blurred.

One of the monsters shrieked, leaping to her feet. The group raced from the building in pursuit of the jeeps.

Wasting no time, I forced myself forward, through the nests and into the alley as gunfire filled the air again. This time we were not the target. Time to run like never before.

Our feet pounded the pavement as we turned each time Lars gave a direction. In the distance, the Ferris wheel rose against the dark sky like a beacon.

"Did we lose them?" I asked.

"They've disposed of the Malignants and have resumed the search. They're two blocks away. Hurry." Urgency laced Lars words. "You cannot let them see you arrive here."

"I know that." Why else were we running through the night, rain threatening? "Just get us clear. Did the others make it?"

"Yes. Turn left, go through that one-story building, then turn right outside and continue forward. You should reach the park in less than five minutes. You've got three monsters creeping up on you."

"Don't stop unless we have to," Fawke said.

"No need to tell me twice." Two humans were a much easier target than three armored jeeps. The Malignant mothers had attacked what they thought a threat without thinking of the dangers. These three wouldn't make the same mistake.

My lungs burned, my legs heavy. I kept my gaze on the wheel and forced myself to go on.

"Let me help you." Fawke put his arm around my shoulders.

"You're tired, too."

"I'm fine." He dragged me along with him. "If we're caught, we're dead."

We stepped onto the park asphalt. Ezra waved to us from the door, pointing behind us.

We whirled as three Malignants leaped.

Ezra sprinted toward us.

I fought to keep the creature's nails and teeth from piercing my skin, while trying to reach the dagger at my waist. In my exhaustion, I was quickly losing the fight.

With a yell, Ezra kicked the creature in the head, only to be attacked by another.

Fawke jumped to his feet, sword in hand and disposed of the one that had attacked him before moving to the one trying to get back at me.

"I've got this one. Help Ezra." I pulled my sword and held it out.

Hungry for the taste of my flesh, the creature impaled itself, driving me backward and flat on my back. I turned my head to keep its blood away from my mouth and drove the sword deeper until it fell off me.

Fawke yanked it away, then turned to help Ezra. One swipe of his sword and the creature's head separated from its body.

A pale Ezra pressed his hand to his shoulder. "I've been bit."

13

After a few short minutes crying in the shower to relieve an almost overwhelming amount of stress, I hurried to the infirmary to check on the three men under Kira's care. A white sheet covered the face of the bit civilian.

"He turned," Kira said, her eyes shimmering. "I had to put him down. The restraints wouldn't hold him."

My mouth dried up. "Two days is all it took." I glanced at Ezra. "You have to save him."

"I'm hoping the medicine will work. It came too late to save Mr. Ardele." She glanced at a sleeping Larsen. "I'm no surgeon, Crynn, but I think I got the bullet out. I wish you could've brought back a real doctor along with the supplies."

Unless one came willingly, that wouldn't happen. I lowered myself into the chair next to Ezra's bed. Sweat poured from his rugged brow. "The fever is broke?"

"It comes off and on. I've done all I can for him. If he isn't better by morning, I'll have to tie him to the bed." Her voice broke. "He's been a part of my life for so long, I can't imagine him gone. I love him." She held his hand to her lips.

"He's strong. He'll be fine." My voice shook. He had to pull through. We needed him. "Where's Fawke?"

"Taking inventory of the things brought back."

Knowing I should help, I couldn't. I had to stay. What if Ezra woke? What if I didn't have the chance to say goodbye to a man who, despite his rough ways, had helped me survive out here?

I rested my forehead against the mattress, barely acknowledging when Gage brought me something to eat. I mumbled a thanks and ate the dry bar of nuts held together with a tasteless paste.

She put a hand on my shoulder. "He'll be okay." Her other hand rested on Ezra's knee.

Nodding, I lifted my head. "He has to." I couldn't imagine life without any of my original group. They were my armor against Soriah's evil.

A far-off rumble had me on my feet. "What is that?"

"Crynn? Control room, please." Dayton's voice held urgency.

"Go," Kira said. "I'll watch Ezra. He's my heart."

I nodded and dashed away, meeting up with Fawke. Together we barged into the control room. Eb hobbled toward us.

"What?" I stared at the monitors.

"The army is decimating the city."

"So that we have nowhere to hide."

"Bombs won't break this place," Eb said. Worry creased his forehead.

"How do you know?" Dayton frowned. "Ever been bombed before? They'll reach us eventually."

"Get everyone in the training room," Fawke ordered. "It's in the center of this place and the strongest room."

Dayton leaned close to the intercom and gave the order.

The infirmary. I whirled and raced to help Kira.

When I entered, Kira struggled with Larsen who insisted on getting to his feet.

"I'm needed to keep people from panicking." He shoved at her hands.

"You can barely walk." Putting her hands firmly on his shoulders, Kira pushed him back to a lying position.

I rushed to Ezra, covering his body with mine as plaster fell from the ceiling.

"As nice as this is, young lady, you plastered against me," he muttered, wrapping his arms around me, "there's a safer place." He rolled with me off the bed and underneath it as the room shook from a well-placed blast.

"Kira! We need to get them to the training room. Ezra, back on the bed, please." I stared into his face. "I can wheel you easier that way." He'd knocked the breath from me, and my ribs ached.

"I have to stay here." Regret filled his eyes. "What if I turn while surrounded by all our people?"

"You won't. You're up and talking. The medicine is working." I crawled from under the bed and tugged at his arm. "We can tie you up if that makes you feel better, but you aren't staying in here."

"Please, Ezra," Kira said, tears running down her

cheeks. "For me."

"You win, ladies." He grunted, getting to his feet. "I expect strong bindings. You can't hurt me anymore than I already am."

"Stop fighting, Larsen," I ordered. "We don't have time for this."

Another bomb hit far too close. I wheeled Ezra from the room as Kira did the same with Larsen.

A short yelp escaped me as another bomb caused a piece of the ceiling to drop in front of us. I sure hope Eb knew what he was talking about regarding the security of this place. Right now, it didn't look hopeful.

Fawke dashed toward us, taking control of Ezra's bed. "You're needed elsewhere, Crynn. The people are panicking. They need your presence to calm them down."

Straightening my shoulders and forcing a brave front I didn't feel, I entered the training room. "Jolt, get their attention, please."

He gave a shrill whistle. "Listen up, people!"

Jenkins moved to my side. "A united front?" He gave a lopsided grin.

"That sounds wonderful."

Fawke and Kira put the patients off to the side and secured Ezra to the bed, covering him with a sheet. Good. If the people couldn't see his bindings, they wouldn't panic more than they already were.

"The army does not know where we are." My voice ricocheted off the walls. "They're bombing aimlessly, destroying potential hiding places. The good news is, they are also killing off Malignants. Eb has guaranteed we are all safe here. We'll wait out this new threat and plan how to proceed once the army has moved on."

"This place could become our grave," someone shouted.

A chorus of agreements rose.

"That will not happen." I met the worried gazes of those in front. "You were not brought here to die, but to live to fight. Please, find a place to relax. This won't last long." I glanced at Jenkins.

"Crynn is right. We are safe here."

His agreement seemed to calm them, and they gathered their families together, huddling against the walls.

The bombs fell closer. Even I wanted to scream. I wanted to run to Fawke and have him gather me in his arms instead of him going around the room comforting others. I wanted to be selfish, cry, scream, anything but pretend a bravado I didn't feel.

For a distraction, I stepped to Ezra's bed. "How are you feeling?"

"Like I got bit. My shoulder burns something awful. My gut hurts. I'm weak as a baby."

"But you're awake and talking. That's good news." I smiled. "Let me see if there is something Kira can do to make you more comfortable."

"Wait. I never told you what a good leader you've been. I want to do that in case…well…you've done far better than I ever thought you could."

I leaned down and kissed his cheek. "That means a lot to me. I've felt insufficient many times."

"You're made of steel, little girl. Now, go find Kira."

My smile widened, and I went in search of Kira.

I found her tending minor cuts from the falling plaster. "Ezra needs something to make him comfortable. He's in pain."

"Thanks to your raid, we have morphine." She put a bandage on a boy's head and went to care for Ezra.

"How is he?" Fawke asked, straightening from where he spoke to a child.

"Better than poor Mr. Ardele. The medicine seems to be working. Did we have a good haul of weapons?"

"Dante filled his pack all with grenades." He grinned. "We have guns and more ammo, even for the machine gun. We did good." He put his arm around my shoulders.

I leaned into him, closing my eyes for a second. He smelled of the soap he'd used in the shower and plaster dust. I breathed deep, releasing some of the fear pent up inside of me.

The bombs fell for over an hour. When they stopped, I headed back to the control room and stared through the monitor at a city unrecognizable. Fires burned bigger. Entire buildings lay in heaps of rubble. The ground marred with craters that could swallow a jeep.

"Some of our cameras were destroyed," Dayton said. "We won't have the same coverage when you go out next time."

"We'll put up more."

"That's the good news. The bad news is both doors are blocked by debris. We're trapped in here."

"Keep that news to yourself. We'll figure it out." I went in search of Eb.

Lights flickered as I marched the halls. I found a very drenched Eb repairing a water pipe.

"Busted. Water will be in short supply until it rains. I'll check the filter next to make sure it's still capable of removing poison from the rain." He placed his hands on his knees and struggled to stand. "Getting up is harder than it used to be."

"Who can I send to help you?" Normally, it would be Ezra.

"Maybe Jenkins has someone skilled in repairs. We need to replaster, someone needs to check the electrical wiring…if we have a fire down here, we're all goners. Let's keep this info to our inner circle." He forced a grin.

"Agreed." I exhaled heavily and went to find him help. After several minutes of searching for Jenkins, I asked Lars, who had traded with Dayton, to find him.

He punched keys on his keyboard. "Dining room."

"Thank you."

I found Jenkins poring over a blueprint of the compound. "You heard?"

"That there's no way out of here? Yeah, I figured as much. You just confirmed."

"Eb needs workers to make repairs, especially an electrician."

"Ha. No need of one on the mountain. Maybe one of the soldiers?" He pointed at the blueprint. "As for an exit, I suggest we check the ones you guys boarded up. See if we can't clear them easier. I can find men to do that." He rolled up the paper.

The soldiers huddled around a different table,

their expressions grave. One of them glanced up as I approached. "How's the sergeant?"

"He's fine. Kira got the bullet out. Are any of you an electrician, plumber, maintenance?"

"We all are. It's part of our training."

"Great. Find Eb. He needs you." I sat in one of their seats as they stood wearier than I could remember. I heard my mother's voice in my head about letting go of stress, that it could wear you down more than anything. That taking a moment to pray worked wonders. I missed her and prayed Soriah hadn't punished her for my rebellion. Maybe not the type of prayer she meant, but it was all I could manage.

Rory sat across from me. "Can I do anything? I feel rather useless around here."

I glanced up. "What can you do?"

"Maybe help Kira? I'm not afraid of blood. Back in Soriah, I helped my mother tend to the medical needs of some of our neighbors. Or I could help in the kitchen. Anything but wander around and make googly eyes at Jolt." She grinned. "Not that I mind that, but I don't feel as if I'm pulling my weight."

"Helping in the infirmary would be wonderful. You don't need to ask my permission to help out."

"How did you get to be leader? You can't be much older than I am."

I explained how I'd been the next to arrive after the prior leader died. "Got lucky, I guess."

"Doesn't sound lucky to me. Too much responsibility. I'm happy staying here instead of going out there where men are sometimes more dangerous than the monsters. The army bombing the city while searching for us proves my point. They don't care if children are harmed. They don't see who the real bad guys are."

She had a very good point. Humans were far more dangerous. With so many Malignants now dead because of the bombing, our biggest threat walked on two legs and carried a gun.

14

After two days, Ezra still hadn't turned, but drifted in and out of consciousness, often running a high fever. Larsen drove everyone nuts with wanting to be on his feet to help clear debris from the exits.

"Please stop acting like a child." Rory planted fists on her thin hips and stomped her foot. "My little sister is less of a pain than you."

"I'm going crazy lying here," the sergeant said.

"Here." Kira pushed a wheelchair into the room. "Compliments of Eb, who like the rest of us, is tired of your complaining."

I smiled from my seat next to Ezra's bed. "Now, go see what kind of trouble you can get into."

"No complaints when I come fetch you to change your bandages." Rory narrowed her eyes.

Larsen grinned. "Not a peep." He slid off the bed and onto the chair. "See ya later, ladies." With a mighty shove, he sent the chair forward, then out the door.

"There's no need to hover, Crynn." Kira placed the back of her hand against Ezra's forehead. "He's out of the worst. He'll make it, thanks to the medicine."

"There's really nothing else for me to do."

"Go help Fawke with the training. That always needs done."

True. I needed to keep my skills honed. I got to my feet and headed to the training room. The sound of clanging swords reached my ears before I entered.

Just as we'd trained in the city, Fawke had everyone paired up. I spotted a few bleeding cuts that would need tended to.

"No sticks?" I arched a brow.

"Don't have any. These are the dullest blades I could find. Besides, the risk of a cut makes them work harder at not getting hit." His eyes sparkled.

"You're brutal." I laughed, watching Roland dance around his opponent as if he'd been wielding a sword his whole life. Sweat poured down the face of the poor man paired up with him.

"Ready to have a go?" Fawke handed me a sword. "I promise to take it easy on you."

"We'll see. Whoever smacks the other in the behind wins." I formed my stance.

In less than five minutes, he laid the flat side of the sword across my rear. "I'm rusty. Two out of three."

He wiggled his fingers. "Bring it."

I took a deep breath and focused, blocking out the sounds of sparring around me. I lunged, twirled, and slid between his legs. I still lost. "Three out of five."

"You'll never be able to best me, sweetheart. I trained you."

"Hmmph." I raised my sword.

"It's your funeral." With an ear-splitting yell he attacked.

I parried.

He swung.

I blocked.

We continued until both of us were breathless and blinded by sweat. "A draw." I grinned.

"No, I won. Easily, but it didn't take you long to remember your training."

"Thank goodness." I swiped my forearm across my eyes. "Want to come with me to check on the progress of the doors being cleared?"

"Sure. Dante and Moses can watch these people." He fell into step beside me. "We'll have a good group of fighters when it's time."

"Enough?"

"There's never enough."

True. The door under the Ferris wheel could not be cleared from the inside. Tons of steel from the ride overhead now lay across the door.

"We got the big door the jeep uses cleared," Eb said. "Took some work, though. We've almost got one of the doors you blocked off when you arrived cleared. Until we can get outside and assess the damage, that's about it."

"Let's give the army a few more days to think they succeeded in finishing us off, then we'll venture out."

Neither Lars or Dayton had seen any sign of soldiers or Malignants since the bombs fell. Outside sensors didn't detect any radiation. I felt fairly certain our location remained a secret. To further keep the secret, I'd ignored Sharon's many attempts at contact. Still, I didn't want to rush and risk exposure.

Next, I peeked into a room where children were schooled. Riva's idea, and Eb had been more than happy to allow her use of the supplies.

"Do you think it's healthy for the children to stay underground all the time?" I glanced at Fawke.

"No, but outside is far more dangerous. There's debris, Malignants, poison rain, all things that could kill off our future generation." He glanced at the ceiling. "Eb's artificial sunlight will have to suffice. Once we topple President Cane from his throne, we can move back to Soriah and expand that city into this one."

A lot of work. "I'd rather move back to the mountain."

"Then that's where we'll go." He turned and headed to the infirmary. "I figured you'd want to check on Ezra."

"I do." I stepped into the room and smiled to see him sitting up. "You look better."

"I feel better." He grinned. "Kira said I can get out of bed for a few minutes if I finish this tasteless broth. Wanna bet it's rat?"

I shuddered. "I know it is."

"Tell me what's been going on?"

I pulled up a chair and told him about the work on the doors, the soldiers repairing broken water pipes and electrical lines. The school for the children, and the ongoing training. "We'll be venturing out in a day or two to assess the outside damage."

"Good. I'll be ready by then." He set his empty bowl on the table next to the bed. "Help me up." He waved Fawke over.

"Five minutes, Ezra. That's all." Kira shot him a stern look. "Or I'll put you in a wheelchair like Larsen."

"Not while I have two good legs, you won't." He grunted as Fawke helped him up. "Just a short stroll down the hall will suffice. I want to feel like I'm still living."

I followed close behind while he leaned on Fawke. It wouldn't be good if he fell and ripped out his stitches. "I think this is far enough."

"I'd like to look at the monitors. I can sit in there."

"Fine." Kira would have my hide for keeping him out longer than she'd said.

Ezra lowered himself gingerly into a chair and stared at the monitors. "They sure did a number on this city. There's hardly any building left standing."

"I haven't seen anything move since the bombing," Lars said. "Either the Malignants are all dead, or they've headed for the mountain."

"Good. That leaves us just the army to deal with." He drummed his fingers on the desk. "We need to go back, start reducing their numbers, crippling them by destroying their equipment."

"How do you propose to do that?" I crossed my arms. "We barely got out of there alive last time."

"Have Larsen come see me. We'll come up with a plan to run by you. Now, get me back to bed before Kira comes looking."

Three days later, I pushed open a side door and stepped outside, only to be stopped by a pile of rubble taller than I was. It would take days to clear more than a few feet in front of the door.

The Ferris wheel lay on top of the compound, providing more camouflage than it had when it stood. The bombs had created more work, but had also served a purpose.

I climbed on top of the rubble and surveyed what had once been a mighty city. Even after the bombing seventy-five years ago, there had been buildings. Now, a wasteland lay before me. Only piles of cement and brick would provide places for anything or anyone to hide. The air stank of rotting Malignant bodies. A thick flock of black birds flew overhead, ready to feast on the carcasses.

I felt more exposed than I had since leaving Soriah. I stared across the expanse in the direction of the army camp. The tips of their white tents shined like stars. We weren't the only ones exposed.

Fawke joined me. "Wow."

"Yeah. Sneaking up on the army will be almost impossible."

"Maybe that was their plan." Fawke lifted a pair of binoculars to his eyes. "They're building a guard tower."

I sighed. Getting in unnoticed would be a huge risk. "Let's see what plan Ezra and Larsen have cooked up. We'll have workers clear this pile under the cover of night."

"That changes things," Ezra said after I told him what we'd seen outside. "We can dress all in black, but getting there unseen…"

"Larsen?" I glanced at the sergeant.

"We'll have to take out the tower with a rocket launcher. Eb said we have a couple. Then, we launch grenades at the camp, destroying as much as we can before attacking. There will be casualties, which I hate, but they won't hesitate to execute any of us if we're caught." He leaned back in his chair. "An aggressive, surprise attack is the only way. Those that survive will know we're still alive, Soriah will send more soldiers, but I don't see another way."

Neither did I. "We go as soon as Ezra is able."

"There are a few military grade riot suits," Eb said, "but not enough for more than ten people. Is that enough? I haven't mentioned them before, because…well, I thought they should be saved for an emergency. This situation counts as one to me."

"It'll have to be enough. If we can get our hands on uniforms when in the camp, do so. It'll take more than one sneak attack, and we'll need every advantage possible. We need their weapons to take down Soriah."

"We can't take down anyone if we all die," Ezra said. "It's a suicide mission, but we all have to die sometime. Might as well die fighting."

"Thanks for the cheering words." Fawke laughed.

"Just being realistic." Ezra reached for a cup of water on the table. "Love up to your women, guys. You might not have another chance."

My face flushed as Fawke cut me a glance. I knew there'd be no loving until this war was over. "We go as soon as a path is cleared outside the door. If we stay lower than the debris, we'll be able to get close enough for the launcher. Fawke, choose the other eight who'll be joining us. Make sure they're prepared."

His gaze lingered for a minute before he turned and left the dining room.

"Why don't y'all get together?" Ezra shook his head. "The tension between the two of you is enough to choke a Malignant."

"Shut up." Laughter followed as I rushed from the room.

I joined several others in the training room and worked off some steam sparring. They weren't as strong a match as Fawke, but I managed to work up a sweat before leaving and joining Lars in the control room.

"We need someone who can install more cameras between here and the army camp. Someone fast. It'll be dangerous, but we need the cameras as close to the camp as possible. Can you formulate the locations and let me know who would be best suited?"

"Sure. I think one of the soldiers would be best since they're trained in installing electronics. I'll study the landscape and see where the cameras would be best suited."

"Thank you." The cameras would be one of the most important things to help us succeed with Larsen's crazy plan.

I headed to my room for the night. Before I could close the door, Fawke stepped inside, closing the door behind him.

His heated gaze caressed my face. "The hell with my stupid resolve. Ezra is right. We might not have another chance." He cupped my face between his hands and lowered his head to kiss me.

15

If I thought moving about the city was tough before the bombing, now it was almost impossible. At least we weren't trying to pull a wagon over and around the piles of rubble.

"Think of it this way," Fawke said. "The jeeps are virtually useless to the army."

I nodded, averting my gaze. After the stormy kiss a few nights ago, and a few other stolen moments when no one was around, I couldn't look at him without blushing like the young girl I'd once been. His kisses were as wonderful as I'd always thought they'd be. Tender, full of longing, sweet beyond imagination.

"Another good thing to point out," Ezra said, pulling me from my thoughts, "is the fact we haven't seen a single living Malignant. Why didn't Soriah bomb this place a long time ago?"

"They did." I faced him. "That's what put us here with the ruined atmosphere, according to Eb at least. It's all about control. They couldn't get us to rid the city and not rebel, so they bombed it again. Just not as bad as before." I'd visited the compound's library a few times and pored over Eb and his father's logbooks. They'd detailed everything from those days long ago.

First, Soriah had destroyed most of the world in order to keep what was left of humanity behind its white walls. Then, as the population grew, they turned their eyes to here. They'd have a heck of a job clearing this place now in order to expand.

I glanced in the direction of the mountain, a yearning to return so strong it weakened my knees. Life could be peaceful there without the threat of Soriah. To gain that, we had a war to fight.

"How close do you want me to get?" Dante asked, the rocket launcher balanced on his strong shoulders.

I glanced at Larsen who I'd wanted left behind because of his limp.

"Half a block more should do it, but we'll have to rush the fence to toss the grenades," the sergeant said. "We'll need to sprint as soon as the rocket is fired. Otherwise, the army will have time to reach their weapons."

"Alright, folks. The sergeant is leading this attack. Follow his orders." I stepped back, letting him take the lead. "You sure you can run on that leg?"

"A little limp won't stop me." He grinned and set off.

I took a deep breath and followed. The taller men stayed hunched, using the cover of rubble as much as possible. With my petite size, most of the piles towered over me. I felt blind.

Larsen stopped us, then motioned for Dante to

use a pile of concrete to rest the launcher on. The rest of us gathered close and waited for the sergeant's order to attack. He counted down on his fingers, three…two…one.

Dante fired.

A direct hit to the tower blew two soldiers into the air.

The rest of us rushed forward, the sergeant falling behind.

I glanced back to see Dante hand him the launcher and take his place in charging the camp. "Fawke, you're in charge now," he said, joining us.

Larsen fired again. Another rocket took out several of the tents used as bunkers.

Shouts of alarm and cries of pain filled the air.

I pulled a grenade from my pack, pulled the pin, and tossed it between two more tents. What didn't explode with the detonation caught fire.

We threw grenades with rapid succession as we sprinted toward the camp. Stop, throw, run. Stop, throw run.

"Hold up." Fawke held up his fist. "Stay together. The fence is gone. You don't want to get in the way of a grenade. Guns out."

I prayed Larsen could tell us from the soldiers and hold off on the rocket launcher. I pulled down my riot mask.

"Where are they?" Someone inside the camp asked. "I thought they were dead."

"Doesn't appear so, Commander," another responded.

I tried to see where the voices came from. Too dark. I ducked behind a jeep, scanning the area for the others. They'd all taken refuge behind vehicles and crates.

I peered over the back of the jeep. Three armed soldiers headed between where I hid and where Fawke had taken cover. I slung my rifle over my shoulder and pulled my sword, Fawke mimicking me.

Lying in wait, I breathed slowly not daring to make a sound. When the soldiers got close, we'd have to dispose of them as quickly and quietly as possible.

The soldiers came within reach. When they passed a few feet from where I hid, I stepped out behind one. "I'm sorry." I whirled, taking off his head as he turned.

Fawke quickly disposed of the other two, not looking any happier at the killing than I felt. He pointed to a stack of wooden crates.

I nodded and followed, taking note of where the rest of our group was. For now, we fought like ghosts, getting closer to the armory tent where I counted five soldiers guarding the flap. I motioned for Dante and Gage to slip around the back. Hopefully, we could keep the soldiers' attention on us while the other two cut the canvas and slipped inside.

"They're here somewhere!" The voice I recognized as the commander's came from somewhere to my right.

I froze, taking cover behind another jeep. Two men now stood in front of the crates Fawke and I had been headed for. If we could get the commander…

A commotion to my left drew my attention. Two

soldiers dragged Larsen between them. A third held the rocket launcher. They shoved Larsen to his knees in front of the commander.

"Lock him up," the commander ordered. "I'll deal with him later."

They dragged Larsen out of sight.

I glanced at Fawke. We had to rescue him. He'd be executed as an example to the other soldiers. That couldn't happen. Not after my vow to leave no one behind.

We couldn't make it to the armory without being seen. I could only pray that Dante and Gage were slipping in and out of that tent to stash weapons somewhere we could retrieve when we finished there.

Fawke made his way to my side. "We need that commander," he whispered.

"Suggestion?"

He shook his head. "We've been here too long as it is."

I agreed and pulled back, motioning to the others to slip away.

Once out of the ruined fence, we skirted around to the back of the armory where a stash of weapons waited. Dante and Gage stood guard, dark scarves wrapped around their faces, nothing visible but the whites of their eyes.

"Anyone know where they keep prisoners?"

"I saw a wagon with bars," Moses said. "We can't save Larsen, Crynn. It'll be heavily guarded."

"I won't leave him. Where's the wagon?"

"Crynn." Fawke put a hand on my shoulder.

I shoved it away. "The rest of you head back with

these supplies. Don't wait for me."

Fawke groaned. "You're the most stubborn person I've ever met. The rest of you go. We'll catch up."

Ezra cursed, then loaded his pack, hefting another launcher onto his shoulder. "You'd better return, little girl." With one last look, he darted away from the camp, the others on his heels.

"Now what, boss?" Somehow Fawke didn't make the title sound like a compliment.

We'd discuss later how I hadn't consulted him before making a decision. Staying in back of the tents, I did my best to spot the wagon. I didn't find it until loud voices drew us to its location.

"Where are they?" The commander stood in front of a wagon holding Larsen. "Are they worth you betraying your president?"

"Yes." A beaten Larsen squared his shoulders. "They don't kill innocent people."

"They've killed soldiers!" He raised a gun and shot Larsen between the eyes.

I raised my gun and fired, taking the commander to his knees. Another shot lay him out. I whirled and ran.

The first shot fired after us grazed my left arm. The second got me in the side.

I fell to my knees.

Fawke slung me over his shoulders as if I weighed nothing and resumed his mad dash to where the others waited. "Go."

No one needed to be told twice.

I groaned at being jostled. "Put me down. I can run."

"In a minute." He stopped behind the protection of a bombed building and set me on my feet. "At least lean on me."

I put my right arm around his shoulders and let him half carry, half drag me away from the camp. "Lars, talk to us."

"You've got five soldiers on your heels. You're going to have to fight. You're moving too slow. There's a concrete wall about thirty yards to your right. Get behind that and be ready. You can easily dispose of them as they pass you."

"Found it." Moses dove over the wall, the others following.

Fawke handed me to him, then leaped over. "Be ready. We shoot, then we run again."

"Anyone else shot?" I asked.

"I am." One of the soldiers who'd joined us slumped against the wall.

I crawled to his side. Blood spread across his midsection. "Hang on. We'll get you to Kira."

"I won't make it. You know it as well as I do."

"Here." Gage handed me a scarf. "Bind your side. He's right. He's a goner."

After tying the scarf as tight around me as I could, I ripped off part of my shirt and bound my arm. "I'm sorry, soldier."

"At least I'll die free." He took a shuddering breath as pounding feet alerted me to the arrival of the enemy.

Gunfire from my group erupted.

"Time to go," Moses said, helping the soldier to his feet. "No man still breathing left behind and all that."

Ezra joined him, propping the soldier between them.

"Lars?" I said.

"You're clear for now, but the camp is stirring. Thanks to the soldier you carry, we have cameras on the army. He got close enough the other night to install several. Looks like they're rallying to come after you with a larger group. You're one block from here. Make haste. I'll let Kira know you've got wounded."

"Do you think the commander is dead?" Dante asked.

"I shot him twice." I put a hand to my side, my heart aching at Larsen's death. The man had been a valuable asset.

The other wounded soldier hung limp between Moses and Ezra. Finally, they propped him against what was left of a building.

"He's gone." Ezra removed the soldier's jacket and lay it over his face. "Rest in peace, warrior."

I wished we could bury our dead, but living out there didn't leave us the luxury of funeral services. We each lay a hand on him in passing and resumed our dash toward safety.

My energy ebbed with each step I took. My grazes bled and the pain threatened to take my breath away. I did my best not to show how bad off I was. I didn't want to slow anyone down, and Fawke would definitely want to carry me again. Either I'd make it on my own or fall.

The Ferris wheel came into sight giving me strength. We'd made it. At least most of us. I'd dwell on our loss later.

Roland stood at the recently cleared door and waved frantically. "Hurry. Soldiers coming."

We made one last race to freedom, Roland slamming the door closed behind us. "Lars said take care of your wounds, then meet him in the control room."

I nodded, letting Fawke help me to the infirmary now that I wouldn't be risking his safety in doing so.

Kira immediately shooed him from the room and started removing my shirt. "The graze on your arm is superficial, but the one across your waist will need stitches. You've lost more blood than I'm comfortable with."

"Just sew me up. I've been summoned." I lay back and closed my eyes against the pain of her ministrations.

Behind my eyelids floated the image of the commander killing Larsen, then me dropping the commander. I hoped I'd killed him, but didn't think my aim had been true. If the man lived, he'd be coming for us harder than ever.

16

After Kira's tending, I moved like an old woman to the control room, sipping a cup of something foul she insisted would help with my blood loss. All I wanted to do was sleep.

"You called?" I slumped into a chair next to Lars.

"Take a look." He pulled up a camera angled toward the white wall of Soriah.

A gate so cleverly designed a person wouldn't know it was there if they hadn't seen it, stood open. Soldiers marched from the city, four of them shoulder-to-shoulder, at least twenty people deep.

The radio on the table flickered. I reached over and turned it away from the wall where I'd focused it so Sharon couldn't tell whether we were dead or alive. Her face appeared on the monitor.

"So, you aren't dead after all." She arched a brow. "Amazing."

"I hope your commander is."

"No, but you did wound him pretty badly, naughty girl. We're sending in reinforcements. You can't hide forever."

The heck we couldn't. "I appreciate your concern, but you really should worry about yourself."

"You don't look good, Crynn. Perhaps you should return to the city and let us care for you. We could use good soldiers like your group."

As if they'd let us live. "I'm not that stupid. If we're not here, who in the world will be left for your army to fight?"

"They're needed rebuilding that city, not destroying it in an effort to locate you." Her face darkened. "President Cane is willing to give you a pardon if you join our army. Stalkers are no longer needed, but strong backs and intelligent minds are."

I glanced to where Fawke listened from the doorway. "You sound desperate, Sharon."

"Crynn?" She disappeared and my mother took her place.

"Mom?" Tears sprang to my eyes. I'd missed her so much. "Are you okay?"

"Now that I know you're alive." She smiled. "Consider the army, dear. I fear for you otherwise."

"I'm alright." I touched the screen, praying she wasn't being hurt in order to convince me to do what Soriah wanted. "I'll think about it."

"That's my girl." She moved out of sight, letting Sharon take her place again.

"Let me know when you've made up your mind. If you live long enough." The screen went dark.

"That woman is full of threats," Lars said. "I wonder what she'd do without those shackles Soriah placed on her."

"Evil is evil." I resumed my seat. "She'd be the

same." I watched the soldiers enter the dark city. "What now?"

Fawke shrugged. "We wait and see what they'll do. We continue our attacks whenever possible. We keep training our fighters."

The same thing every day until one of us wins. I groaned and got to my feet, draining the rest of the medicine in my cup. "I'm going to bed."

I waved off Fawke's attempt to help me and made my way, collapsing onto my bunk. Could I really keep fighting? We lost someone every time we encountered Soriah's army. As outnumbered as we were it was a matter of time before they won. Could I keep risking lives?

Not to fight meant a lifetime underground. I didn't want that either.

I spent a restless night. Turning on either side pulled at my stitches. The graze on my arm burned. After five hours, I crawled from bed and shuffled to the infirmary.

"In pain?" Rory's eyes widened. "All we have is morphine."

"I don't want that." I sighed and sat. I'd hoped for a pill or something. "I guess you can check my bandages." While she worked, I concentrated on how my mother had looked. Healthy. Not injured. I could only hope she'd stay that way as I continued my rebellion.

The roof shook again. I bolted to my feet.

"More bombs," Fawke called, rushing past the infirmary.

I followed at a much slower pace as the people once again gathered in the training room.

"Looks like they believe we're underground somewhere," Eb said. "This place will hold. Don't worry. There's nothing they can do worse than what has happened before."

My fear wasn't that it wouldn't, but that the things over us that kept us hidden would be discovered. "Can they cut off our water and electricity?"

"No. My father made sure of that. Everything is buried and disguised." Eb leaned heavily on his cane.

"Crynn and Fawke to the control room." Dayton called.

I shuffled that way in time to see a soldier racing across the amusement park grounds. Bullets kicked up dust at his feet as he zig-zagged. "A deserter?"

"Possibly." Fawke leaned over my shoulder. "Or a ruse to get us to open our door and reveal ourselves."

"I think you're right." Dayton pulled up another camera view to reveal the same scenario with a different soldier. "They're hoping we'll have pity and open a door. They have no idea where we are. I've spotted at least five fleeing soldiers in different areas of the city. They know we accept deserters."

"Not those five." I sat and stared at the five different soldiers.

With as much gunpower firing around them, they should be nothing but mincemeat by now. The gunners missed on purpose.

The soldiers found hiding places, cowering behind rubble. The shooting seized and bombing resumed, staying conveniently away from the areas where the hiding soldiers were. Nice try, Soriah.

"How many cameras do we have left to replace any damaged this time?" I asked.

"Three. Then, we're out." Dayton crossed his arms. "So far, we're good. They don't seem as determined to flatten anything this time, just draw us out."

The bombing lasted less than an hour. A futile attempt at frightening us into coming out.

"Let them stew for a few days, and we attack again." I stood. "Let them guess as to whether they got us this time."

The rest of the day we spent in minor repairs before I sat and supervised training. With my injuries, I wasn't good for much else. Boredom quickly set in, allowing my mind to dwell on what life would be like if we did turn ourselves in. Would prison or laborers be worse than the constant fighting? No, freedom would always be better.

"What's wrong?" Fawke, arms crossed, frowned down at me. "You're avoiding me."

"Not really. Just working through some things in my mind."

"Mind sharing? I thought we were a team."

"We are. Sorry about insisting we go back for Larsen."

His gaze softened. "You paid the price, almost getting killed. Too bad you didn't finish off the commander." He pulled up a chair to sit beside me. "Are you considering Sharon's offer?"

"Absolutely not. It crossed my mind, but she can't be trusted. She'd have all our heads on a stake and the children in an orphanage. We have to stick it out."

"We'll lose people."

I narrowed my eyes. "I know that. Are you wanting to turn yourself in?"

"Nope." He grinned. "Just making sure you've thought it through."

"I have. I want to give these people the option to stay or go, but anyone allowed to leave could give away the location of this place. It can't be risked."

"They were all on that mountain for a reason." He put his hand over mine. "They could have gone to Soriah at any time and chose not to. None of them will surrender."

"What about when we storm Soriah? That day will come."

"They know the risk. That's what they're training for. Keep your eyes on the prize, Crynn. A life without Soriah's tyranny."

I leaned my head on his shoulder, relishing in his warmth when his arm snaked around me. "I try, but the doubts still come."

"You're doing great." He kissed the top of my head and stood. "Back to work. I'll see you later."

I returned to the control room, the only job I could do with stitches in my side. "Go take a break," I told Dayton. "I got this."

"I'll bring your lunch." He flashed a grin and left me to watch the dark, desolate landscape.

The fires burned less with every bomb dropped. Soon, the gases would burn out, leaving the place colder and darker than ever. That could work to our advantage. We knew this city. The army didn't. Without the fires lighting the way, we might be able to slip into the camp easier.

I studied the monitor depicting the camp. Soldiers milled around like ants. Useless jeeps sat like discarded toys. Newly erected tents took the places of the ones we'd destroyed. Several soldiers worked at erecting a new fence. This time out of the piles of rubble rather than chain link.

I laughed. I'd scaled those piles many times as agile as a monkey. The piles would take less time to scale than cutting the fence.

I sobered as two soldiers started laying booby traps. I grabbed a sheet of paper from a small stack next to the monitors and did my best to draw a rudimentary map of the make-shift fence and where the traps were sent. I peered close, noting any brick or block different than the others to use as a landmark in what I hoped would help us get over the top without mishap.

"What are you doing?" Dayton handed me a freeze-dried meal ration, curtesy of our latest raid.

"They're setting traps. I'm marking them down."

"Genius. You should've been an army commander." He laughed. "Guess you kind of are. Strange for such a young girl."

"Didn't have a choice." I bit into the dry bar, thankful I ended up having what it took whether I wanted it or not.

"Crynn?" Jenkins entered the room. "Got a minute?"

"Sure." I turned my chair to face him.

"Folks are bored and restless. There isn't enough for them to do. On the mountain, we had gardens, hunting…"

"We have clothing that needs washed and

mended, rooms to be cleaned, Eb could use help in the garden. There's plenty of things to do."

"I think they want assigned jobs. It's what they're used to."

"Alright. I'll find out what needs done on a regular basis, then you and I will decide who does what. Give me a few hours."

"Welcome to the world of community," he said. "Everyone wants something that makes them feel as if they're contributing."

"Then, we'll make sure they have what they need." I grabbed another sheet of paper and started visiting different sections of the compound. The people weren't the only ones who needed to stay busy underground.

Within a few hours, I had a list of jobs and met up with Jenkins in the dining room. He placed names next to all the jobs.

"This will make the people happy. Life is different underground, but there are still things that need doing," he said.

"I agree. The fighters will need to attend all training sessions in-between their work. That's non-negotiable."

He nodded. "I'll let them know. As for me, I've joined the sessions. I'm going to fight when the time comes."

"No. You'll be needed here in case something happens to me."

"I won't stay behind. This is my world we're fighting for."

"Eb will need you. He's old." I refused to back down. "With the risks I take out there, we can't both fight."

"Then you stay back."

"When you came, I told you I was the leader. You agreed. Are you disobeying a direct command?"

His eyes flashed. "No, but you're being unreasonable. I'm able bodied."

"If this place is discovered, you'll fight then. Until that happens, you look over the survivors in my absence." I left the room, leaving him to fight with himself.

If something happened to me, Fawke was more than capable of stepping into the role of leader. He was definitely more qualified than me. But if something happened to us both, Jenkins would be needed.

17

"You aren't ready for another attack." Fawke glared at me, arms crossed. "You still have stitches not fully healed."

"I'm going stark raving mad here." I glowered. "I'm fine."

Eb shuffled into the dining room. "Crynn, Fawke, follow me, please."

I shot Fawke a questioning glance, then headed after Eb. He led us to the gardens.

"The latest bombing shattered some of the light bulbs. I never thought I'd say this, but if we can't find replacements, we will run out of food."

My heart sank. "Do we have any more stored somewhere?"

"There should be a crate full, but I can't find them."

"How many helpers do you need?" This sounded like an emergency to me. I'd spare anyone.

"Maybe ten of the teenagers, if they can give up training for a day or two."

"You'll have them." I turned and went in search

of Jenkins, letting him know of our need.

"Long, skinny bulbs?" His gaze searched the training room. "I'll get a group searching."

Since I'd been all over that compound in our first days there, I took two of the boys with me, Fawke doing the same. Dante and Ezra were more than capable of overseeing the training, and I needed something to do.

"Grab one of those crowbars." I pointed to a stack in the corner of the room Eb kept tools. "Open every crate you see except the metal sealed ones. Those only contain food." I noticed there were a lot fewer of them than there used to be. What would we do with only rats to eat?

Although the tool room seemed the most likely place for bulbs, we found none. We next searched the garage full of useless vehicles.

"Crynn to the control room."

I sighed. "You boys keep looking. They're here somewhere. Take them straight to Eb when you find them." Be careful what you wish for, my mother always said. I'd complained about boredom and now ran from one place to the next as if I had no clue what I was doing.

"What is it?" I sat in the chair next to Lars.

"Group of civilians. Looks like mostly women and children, a couple of men."

Since the fires had stopped burning, I could barely make out the group in the night's darkness. "Another decoy?"

"I don't think so. The army wouldn't use women and children. Too much of a liability. They'd only slow things down. Besides, look how loaded down they are."

Even the children wore bulging backpacks. They couldn't be left for the army to find, then. "Find Fawke. We're going out. Fifteen minutes at the back door."

"Alone?"

I nodded. "Two will move faster. Keep your eyes on us." I slid my earpiece in place. The dark would work to our advantage.

"I'll guide you every step of the way for as long as I can. Good luck."

I hurried to my room for my sword, stopped at the armory, then raced to the door where Fawke would meet me. I tapped my foot as time ticked away.

"Found the bulbs." A teen darted past me. "Headed to the garden."

One problem solved, at least. The quietness of the compound as its residents returned to their rooms and a night's sleep, calmed my racing heart. Were people actually fleeing Soriah? It was too much to hope for.

The compound was large, but we'd fill up. I shook off the worry. We'd take every person who no longer wanted under President Cane's rule.

"I'm here." Fawke hurried toward me, sheathing his sword.

I told him of the group of civilians. "Ready?"

He nodded and opened the door.

I stepped out and climbed over the rubble I'd insisted stay to help hide the entrance. A path would've been noticeable to anyone taking a second glance.

A searchlight lit up the sky.

I ducked, glancing at Fawke. "When did the army install that?"

"No idea, but it isn't good for us."

Or the civilians. I sighed and clambered over the top, jumping to the ground, then ducked as the light swept across the area again. This would take a long time.

"Talk to me, Lars."

"The civilians are holed up under a building toppled over and lying on top of another. Looks like they're staying put because of that damn light."

"Any sign of soldiers?"

"Not yet."

Fawke and I would sprint forward when the light shined away, then duck when it swung back, making slow progress toward the group we searched for. "How will we get them back unseen?"

"We'll have to wait until morning," he said.

When the possibility of patrolling soldiers increased. I preferred them over the light. They were easier to escape from.

"Turn left at the first opportunity," Lars said. "Toward the open field. Skirt along the edge until I say to stop. The rubble is higher there. The light won't catch you."

Less than a block. We could do this.

Hunching over despite the pulling on my stitches, we headed in the direction Lars had told us to go. The trek took far longer than it should have.

I tripped while ducking and fell to my knees.

Fawke helped me up. "You should rest."

"Listen."

In the distance came a baby's cry.

"If we can hear that, it's only a matter of time before the army does. We can't stop to rest." I wasn't sure how to quiet a crying infant, but…

He waved me forward. To appease him, I slowed my pace. Next time I might fall and hit my head.

We reached the field. Lars was right. The rubble was tall enough to hide us. I started to run again. "Where, Lars?"

"About three buildings down. You'll see one lying on top of another. They're in there."

The baby had hushed, leaving us to rely on Lars' instructions rather than sound.

"There." Lars pointed to a tall building, cut in half by the bombs. The top half lay on top of a shorter building.

We jumped inside seconds before the searchlight turned toward us.

A woman whirled, a dagger in her hand.

"Mom?" Was it really her? "What are you doing out here?"

"Oh, thank you." She dropped the dagger and wrapped me in her arms. "The moment I found out you were still alive, I made plans to leave that place. They were pressuring me to do anything I could to get you to turn yourself in."

I glanced at her left hand, shocked to see she missed two fingers. "They were torturing you?"

"They stopped when I spoke to you on the radio. Thank God you found us. These are the only people in Soriah I trust." She smiled at the group of eight women, two men, and five children. "It's been quite the hike."

"How did you get out?" I still couldn't believe

she stood in front of me.

"Rupert knows a secret passage." She introduced a man who looked to be around fifty. "That's how your army will get in and take down the president."

"When we're ready. This is Fawke. He helps me lead those in the compound." I hugged her again. "We have to wait until morning to leave here. Please, keep the children quiet. We can't chance the army finding us."

"I am so proud of you." She caressed my face. "Sit. You look exhausted. We've food and water, medical supplies. No weapons other than knives, I'm afraid. We couldn't be conspicuous. One of us is lost out there. She fell, and we couldn't chance finding her."

"Just you being here is enough for me." I sat on a cracked cement block.

Fawke moved to where he could keep watch outside. "Get some rest, people. The trip tomorrow won't be easy with little ones."

The last thing I wanted to do was sleep. I sat next to Mom and told her everything that had happened since my arrival here.

"You've had a tough time." She gripped my hand. "You've your father's bravery."

"I haven't always felt brave. Sometimes it's sheer stubbornness that keeps me going."

She chuckled. "Whatever it takes." She leaned her head against the wall. "I can't believe you've survived."

"I've had help." I glanced at Fawke. "And others." I told her about the group I'd arrived with and those who came after.

"Hopefully, there is a place for us. Rupert is a surgeon. Millie, a seamstress. The others all have skills they can contribute."

"That makes two seamstresses." I remembered the fine gowns my mother sewed for those on the hill. "Fabric is something we lack here in Rebel City."

"There's always a way." Still holding my hand, she closed her eyes. Within seconds she snored.

"Sole woman stumbling about half a block from you," Lars said. "She looks injured."

Fawke glanced back at me.

"Go."

He darted out.

I didn't worry. He'd stay out of sight of the search light. If the woman could be found, he'd find her with Lars' help. I wasn't letting go of my mother's hand for a while. My eyes drifted closed.

They snapped open as Fawke, his arm around a limping woman, joined us. "Crynn, meet my mother."

I rushed to help him. "What happened?"

"My foot slipped into a hole. I think my ankle is broken."

"Why would these people leave you behind?" He helped her sit, then knelt in front of her. "I need something to bind her ankle."

I nodded and found a scarf among the others' belongings.

"I told them to. That stupid light stayed right on our heels. We couldn't put the group in danger. It was easy enough for me to blend in with the rubble." She cupped her face. "You silly boy. Rebelling so close to the end of your term."

153

"I had to." He glanced at me.

"Ah. I see." She smiled in my direction. "The infamous Crynn Dayholt. The girl who keeps Soriah on their toes." She hissed as Fawke bound her ankle. "Those in authority in the white city are quite upset with you."

I smirked. "What does the black square on the wheel mean now?"

"Work in the mines. Things are rough in Soriah. Fuel is in short supply, space even shorter. They need this city, and your little group is in their way."

Rupert took Fawke's place. "Let me look, Anna. You didn't say anything, just fell behind."

"Couldn't slow the rest of you down."

I could see where Fawke got his strength.

"It's definitely broken," the doctor said. "I can't do anything more out here. Rest."

When everyone slept except me and Fawke, we moved back to where we could see outside. "How many more do you think will come?" I asked.

He grinned down at me. "I think many. As things get worse in the city, the president will start saving food and water for the rich. The poor will suffer. That will make them desperate. We'll get our army, Crynn." He took my hand in his. "You wait and see. They'll come."

So would the traitors. Once Soriah figured out what was happening, they'd send someone they could trust. Someone who would betray us.

A friendly face could turn out to be anything but a friend.

I glanced at the group behind us. It could even be one of them. Someone my mother trusted. Someone who could gain access to the radio in the control room and let Sharon know where we were.

"We'll have to blindfold them."

"It'll take three times as long to get to the compound."

"I know, but we can't risk any more people knowing where the compound is."

He nodded, his jaw set, and returned his attention to the outside. "Hopefully, I'm right about the searchlight not being on during the gray hours of the day."

18

Black faded and gray took its place. I gathered the newcomers together. I'd lead with Fawke and his mother taking the rear.

"Don't wait for us," he said. "I'll get her there. You worry about the others."

"You'd better make it." I cupped his face and kissed him, long, hard, desperate.

With a sigh, he pulled back and rested his chin on my head. "Focus on these people. I'll care for my mother."

I peered into his face. "She hasn't been tortured, why?"

"Since Sharon hasn't seen me on the monitor, they most likely think I'm dead. They aren't sure which of the Stalkers are still alive except for you." He smiled. "That could work in our favor. Now, go." He stepped back.

I wanted to tell him all the emotions roiling through me, but knew he wouldn't welcome the words of love. I could see his feelings in his eyes. He'd hold them in until we were free.

I turned to the others. "We move fast and quiet. Copy my every move. Lars?"

"Coast is clear. Head back the same way you went."

With a nod, I stepped out of our shelter and looked both ways. Not seeing anyone coming or the beam of the searchlight, I waved the others forward.

The trek along the edge of the field went easy. Once we hit rubble, it was stop, climb over, hand over an infant, move on and repeat.

I glanced back, grimacing at the agony on Anna's face as she leaned on Fawke. She'd propped an iron bar under one arm as a crutch.

"Don't wait for us." Fawke scowled. "Move on."

My heart tore in two, part wanting to get my mother to safety, the other wanting to stay behind with Fawke. I took a deep breath and continued forward, leaving part of me behind.

"Soldiers about two blocks behind you," Lars said. "Just came into view. No idea where they were hiding."

"How many?"

"Five. Looks like a scouting mission."

I urged the group to move faster and fell back to speak to Fawke. "Soldiers coming."

"My mother and I will hide. We'll never outrun them."

I gripped his hand. "I'll stay with you. The others can make it without me."

"No." His gaze hardened. "I can't worry about both of you." He pointed to a hollowed out single-story structure. "We'll hole up in there. Once the soldiers are gone, we'll continue."

"Food and water?" My voice cracked.

"In my pack," Anna said. "We'll be fine. Get the children to safety."

Tears pricked my eyes as I hurried to catch up to the others. I'd vowed to never leave anyone behind, and now I left the man I loved. I'd be back as soon as these people were underground.

I glanced back and caught no sight of Fawke or his mother. He knew this city. They'd be safe. They had to be.

Bombs started to fall as we neared the fields. "Into the grass! Run as far as you can."

Women screamed.

Babies cried.

I whirled toward where I'd left Fawke. "Fawke!"

I ducked as debris flew. *Please, God.* Back upright, I bolted into the grass trying to get as far away from the city as possible, scooping up a child who couldn't keep up on my way.

The army didn't seem concerned about the fields, focusing on what was left of the city. I put my arm around my mother and cowered as low to the ground as possible. Fear for Fawke and Anna choked me.

"Lars, do you see him?"

"No. The soldiers are headed back to their camp at a run. I don't think they were supposed to be out there."

Deserters maybe. Returning to a camp that was safer than bombs?

"Let me know as soon as you spot them."

"Roger that."

When the bombing stopped, I ordered everyone to their feet. "We run."

Time was of the essence. We couldn't hide forever in the grass, and we couldn't wait to see if more bombs would fall. Safety lay under that giant Ferris wheel in the distance. The sooner we reached sanctuary, the sooner I could return to search for Fawke.

We arrived at the compound mid-day. I handed everyone into the capable hands of Jenkins. "I have to go back, Mom. I need to find him."

Concern clouded her features. "I know, dear."

"Not without us." Ezra and the rest of my original group arrived, all fully armed. "He's our friend, too."

"Kira…"

"There's a doctor here now. Rory can assist." She hitched her chin, handing us each a pack with food and water.

"To take our best fighters—"

"One of our best is out there," Dante said.

"The bombs…"

Ezra smirked. "The army has never bombed more than once in a day."

I had no more arguments, and I'd never loved these people more than I did in that moment. "Let's go."

We were a solemn group leaving through the back door. If their thoughts were anywhere near as macabre as mine, they all suspected the worst. That Fawke and his mother had perished. That we'd find pieces of them or their bodies buried under rubble. Still, we had to know one way or the other.

Lars refused to take a break and let Dayton take over. "I've not seen signs of anything moving out there. Could be more bombs coming. Be careful."

"Focus on the army camp. We're counting on you."

"I can't see when they fire. The bombs are coming from out of camera range. I'll do my best, though."

We found the five dead soldiers before reaching where I'd seen Fawke last. They might have run toward camp but had somehow gotten turned around and now lay crushed under a ton of cement.

"Fawke is smarter than these guys," Ezra said, putting a hand on my shoulder. "He's fine."

I nodded, glancing to where I'd last seen him and his mother. From that distance, I couldn't tell whether their shelter had been hit.

We salvaged what we could from the soldiers and continued forward.

"Got my eyes on Fawke and his mother," Lars said. "That's the good news. Bad news is there are soldiers heading right for them. The non-deserting kind. Heavily armed."

"Can you warn them?" My blood ran cold.

"Negative. He isn't responding."

I groaned and increased my pace. We needed to reach them before the soldiers did.

The building they'd hid in came into sight as I climbed over a pile of rubble.

Fawke helped his mother limp our way.

The soldiers came into sight and raised their guns to fire.

I dove off the rubble as Fawke turned, his hands held high.

I peered over the pile of shattered concrete and cracked blocks as the soldiers converged on Fawke and his mother. Seconds later, they were marched toward the army camp.

No! I went to clamber back over the rubble in front of me.

Ezra wrapped his arms around my waist and lifted me off my feet. "Running out there all crazy won't save him."

"They'll kill him."

"Not unless they find out he's a Stalker. He's smart. He'll think of something."

I wrenched free, whirling to glare up at him. "We can't leave him."

"No, we can't. But we'll have to wait until dark. It won't do him any good if we're all caught, especially you." He crossed his arms. "If they catch you, they'll kill you on the spot. You're the one these people are counting on to lead the rebellion."

"Someone would take my place if I were killed."

"And they'd become the new target."

Ugh. I transferred my attention back to where Fawke and his captors grew smaller and smaller. Fine. We'd wait for dark, but I wouldn't return to the compound without him.

Ezra found an alcove for us to wait out the last remaining hours of daylight. I nibbled on a dry piece of meat. My gaze kept flicking toward the army camp. What were they doing to him and Anna?

I hadn't seen his sword or gun. I got to my feet. "I'm going to check out where Fawke had been hiding."

"Why?" Gage frowned. "You're going to get us caught."

"I think he left his weapons behind."

"Why would he do that?"

"So, he could pass himself off as something other than a Stalker," Moses said. "Brilliant, really. All him and his mother had on them were packs. They could easily pass as scavengers. I doubt Soriah has stopped sending them even with the bombings. Scavengers are the lowest of the low and expendable more than anyone."

We gathered up our things and, staying low, made our way to where Fawke and his mother had hid. We found his weapons behind some blocks lying in the corner.

"He must have seen the soldiers coming and knew if he were caught with guns they'd kill him on the spot," Dante said. "So, he stepped out as if he were leaving this place."

Made as much sense as anything. I added his weapons to my pack and settled in to wait another hour until nightfall.

When darkness fell, we headed to the barricade. I warned everyone to step where I stepped. I pulled the map of booby traps I'd drawn from my pack and squinted. Please don't let me make a mistake.

Our primary goal was Fawke and his mother. If we had the opportunity to grab supplies, we would, but not so much it would weigh us down. Hopefully, our friends weren't being held in the wagon Larsen had. Getting to them would be almost impossible.

I placed my foot on the first block and marked an X with a piece of chalk. When I didn't set off a trap, I took another, then another.

The others followed in a single line.

Someone's foot dislodged a rock. I froze, the

sound loud in the night. When no cries of alarm or explosion came, I continued down the other side, using a tent as coverage to block the view of anyone looking.

Once everyone joined me, we hunkered down behind the tent. Now what? I couldn't see the wagon. If Fawke wasn't there, where would they hide him? I pointed toward the infirmary.

Ezra nodded, taking the lead. He'd dispose of any doctor on duty, then wave the rest of us forward.

I held my breath as he darted forward, only releasing it when he waved us on. With the others staying back, I ducked into the tent. Anna, a cast on her leg, lay on a cot, eyes wide.

"Where is he?" I whispered.

"I don't know. They beat him, then dragged him away. They tried to get him to tell them where we're hiding. He told them we were all that was left after the bombing, but they don't believe him." Tears flowed down her pale cheeks.

"Get her out of here, Ezra. Send Gage and Kira to get supplies from in here. Send Dante to help me. The rest of you head back. Our group is too large to slip through this camp unseen. Step only on the marked path when you head back."

He didn't look happy, but nodded. "We'll meet up where we waited out most of the day."

"No, we'll meet back in the compound. Lars will keep us all updated on where each other is." I couldn't rescue Fawke if I worried about everyone else. "Go. Before we're discovered."

I grabbed a couple of uniforms folded on the foot of an empty cot and tossed one to Dante before pulling the pants and shirt over my clothes. Dante didn't need help looking larger, but I would never pass for a soldier without extra padding.

Back outside, I waited in the shadows for Dante to join me. "Girl, that blond hair of your's is like a beacon." He slapped his hat on my head. "All they can see of me is my eyes and teeth. You might want to wipe off those stripes you insist on painting on your cheeks."

I chuckled, rubbing the stripes away with my sleeve. "Then don't smile. Ready to go hunting?"

"Live for it."

Dante led the way. We stopped at the back of a tent and softly called for Fawke. No answer.

We turned the corner to see the empty jail wagon.

A few tents further on, I froze. My blood ran cold.

Tied to a post in the center of camp hung a shirtless Fawke, his hands chained over his head. Even from that distance I could see the whip marks on his back, the blood soaking the waistband of his pants.

19

I sagged against Dante. "Is he…?"

"Dead? I don't think so." He put his hands on my shoulders. "Straighten up. We have to march out there like we're assigned the task of taking him off the post."

Nodding, I squared my shoulders. Fawke needed a warrior not a weeping willow.

Dante nodded to a passing guard. The soldier barely spared us a glance as he headed to his post.

The army obviously didn't expect a raid. Not with traps set around the perimeter.

"Oh, Fawke." The damage to his back looked worse than I'd thought. Ground meat would be the most apt description. I reached for the rope keeping his arms around the pole.

"What are you doing there?" A soldier marched toward us. "I thought the sergeant said to leave him until morning."

I moved to the opposite side of the pole and kept my head down.

"The sergeant changed his mind. Said the

prisoner needs medical attention for my questioning in the morning. Can't get answers out of a dead man," Dante said.

The soldier laughed. "True enough. I look forward to more questioning." His boots crunched as he moved away.

"We've got to hurry." Dante pulled a knife from his belt and sliced the ropes, then propped his shoulder under Fawke's arm. "Crynn, you'll have to keep a watch. We'll head toward the infirmary, then around the back."

"I'll tell you where to place your feet when we cross the barricade." I marched in front of them, head up, shoulders squared, doing my best to act as if I obeyed orders.

At the medical tent, I glanced back. Not seeing anyone, I led the way around the tents to where we'd entered the camp. "Careful," I whispered. I could barely make out the chalk marks we'd placed earlier. "Step where I step."

Fawke groaned, but didn't open his eyes.

One careful placement of our feet after another. I didn't breathe easy until all three of us stood on firm ground.

We couldn't stop to rest. Couldn't find a place to hide. Once the sergeant discovered we hadn't gone to the infirmary, we'd have soldiers on our tails.

"Head east," Lars said. "The others are waiting for you."

While glad we were now in range of his voice, I wasn't happy the others hadn't gone ahead. "Doesn't anyone follow orders?"

"Anna wouldn't leave without her son."

I heaved a heavy sigh and turned east. I couldn't blame her. I'd gone back for him after all.

When we caught up with them, Ezra took Fawke from Dante and lowered him onto a makeshift travois. He gripped the two poles and jerked his head forward. "Best get moving. Dante, grabbed the one with Anna."

With our two injured being carried, we headed in the direction of home. I constantly glanced at Fawke, reassured by the gentle rising of his chest. *Hold on. Please hold on.*

Kira put a hand on his chest, then gave me a trembling smile. Probably meant to be reassuring, but had the opposite effect. We had several blocks to go, two people who needed carrying, and an army that would come searching. The odds were not in our favor.

"Anyone coming?" I asked Lars.

"Not yet. If you make it back before dawn, you should be good."

A few blocks never seemed so long before. Leaving Fawke in Kira's capable hands, I fell back, taking up the rear. With Fawke out of commission, I was the strongest fighter if we were attacked. We hadn't seen a Malignant in days, so I wasn't too concerned.

"Two soldiers coming up fast," Lars said.

Only two? I ordered the others to keep going and turned to wait, sword in my hand.

As usual, they didn't listen. Everyone except Ezra and Dante who pulled the travois took up a fighting stance. "I thought I was the leader." I scowled.

"We've decided to choose when to obey." Moses laughed.

I rolled my eyes. "Stop."

The two soldiers stopped, their hands in the air. I recognized one of them as the man who had questioned us at the post.

"We want to come," he said. "I'm Private Stanley, Stan for short. This is Morrison."

"How do we know you aren't spies?" Gage asked.

"Because I could have cried out an alarm back there and didn't." Stan stared us down.

True. He hadn't given us away. "You'll have to be blindfolded."

"That's fine. Just let us go with you."

I motioned my head for Gage to blindfold them. "Jolt, Moses, you lead them. Let's go."

"Are you sure?" Moses frowned.

"He didn't give us away." My gut told me we could trust them. "Lars?"

"You're all clear."

It didn't take long to catch up to the others. The first rays of weak sunlight appeared over the horizon as the Ferris wheel came into view.

Since we had the travois, the big door lowered, allowing us easy access. I ordered the two soldiers to the cell and followed as Fawke was carried to the infirmary.

The doctor clicked his tongue as he rolled Fawke onto his stomach. "Nasty work. I'll get him patched up, but he'll bear some nasty scars. He'll be out of commission for a while."

But he'd live. That's all I cared about. I

reluctantly left him and headed to my room for a few hours of sleep.

When I woke, I headed straight to the infirmary, asking that breakfast be brought to me, and sat in a chair beside Fawke's bed.

His eyes fluttered open. "No man left behind."

I smiled, gripping his hand. "Absolutely right. How do you feel?" In the light, his face sported bruises, one eye almost swollen shut.

"Like I've been beaten. Like someone poured fire on my back."

"The medicine I used probably did feel like that," the doctor said, looking under a cloth soaked with a strong smelling antiseptic. "No bones broken. You're lucky there, although there is some bruising of your ribs."

"I don't think there's an inch of me that isn't bruised or cut, but I'm still breathing, and for that I'm grateful." His gaze settled on me. "Kira said you brought back two deserters."

"Yes. One of them saw us cutting you down and didn't turn us in. They're locked in the cell for now." I rubbed my thumb across the back of his hand. "Maybe they can give us some information on the camp or Soriah's plans."

"I'll question them in a day or two." Fawke's eyes drifted closed seconds after the doctor gave him a shot.

Rory brought me breakfast. "Eggs from a military ration packet. Freeze dried. Yummy."

I laughed. "I'm hungry enough to eat anything, but I don't need special treatment."

"Today you do. You had a rough night worrying

about your man." She patted my shoulder and left.

"You love him." Anna smiled from across the room. "He'll be fine, you know? My son is a strong man."

"You must have missed him."

"Very much. I'd looked forward to him coming home." She stared at the bowl of gruel in front of her. "It would have been a few months from now." She sighed and picked up her spoon. "Still, I chose to leave Soriah. Things are bad there."

"You would have lived a life of luxury when he returned."

"No. Things are not the same. They aren't letting anyone else live on that hill. They've started hoarding food, water, fabric, even the manufactured sunlight. Those down the hill spend most of their day in dimness." Her gaze pierced mine. "They need this city."

"Then why bomb it?"

"Because it serves two purposes. Kill you and clear the city." She shrugged. "I'm sure they didn't want to destroy all the buildings, hence the need for Stalkers, but when you failed them, they didn't have any other choice."

"How do you know this?" My fork paused halfway to my mouth.

She smiled. "I cleaned the palace rooms. The other maids talk a lot, they hear things."

Then getting others to leave the white city shouldn't be too hard. The problem would be getting in. I glanced at Fawke willing him to wake so we could formulate a plan.

A red flush colored his cheeks. I placed the back

of my hand against his forehead. "He's burning up. Kira!"

She rushed into the room, checked him, then hurried back out, returning with the doctor.

Rupert shook his head. "I'd hoped he wouldn't get an infection." He pulled a syringe from a drawer. "We'll have to keep a close watch on him for the next day or two." He plunged the needle into Fawke's arm.

An urge to do the same to whoever had whipped him took my breath away. How many lashes until they realized he'd never talk? Would they have moved to Anna then in order to loosen Fawke's tongue?

I bolted to my feet, hungry to find something to work off my anger. "I'm going to the training room."

Once there, I scanned the room for someone to spar with. Someone skilled enough to make me sweat, to exhaust me.

"What's wrong?" Dante marched to my side.

"Fever." I took a deep breath through my nose.

"He'll fight it off."

I narrowed my eyes. "Want to spar?"

He widened his eyes. "I have a feeling you'll kill me. Let's go hunting instead."

"For what?" I forced the question through gritted teeth.

"Soldiers, Malignants…"

"We haven't seen a Malignant in days."

"Lars spotted three on the cameras."

A manageable size. I grinned, the feel of my sword in my hand. "Let's go."

We headed for the armory, then slipped out the

back door. Only Lars knew we left and would guide us to the beasts' hiding place. Eliminate and return.

Dante sent me several worried glances. "You're going up and over the rubble like a mountain goat. Slow down. Haste makes mistakes."

My shoulders slumped. "I feel helpless."

"Fawke will be okay. You survived the Malignant wound, remember? You aren't nearly as tough as he is." His teeth flashed.

"Point made." I grinned.

"If the two of you are finished talking," Lars said. "You've got Malignants climbing over the next pile in front of you. Might want to get rid of them before the soldiers two blocks away catch sight of you."

"How many soldiers?"

"Five and one rocket launcher. They don't appear to be searching for anything. A scouting party most likely."

The Malignants spotted us and shrieked.

I lifted my sword over my head and advanced.

Dante pulled a shorter sword and a dagger.

The Malignants weren't full grown and disposing of them didn't quite release as much tension as I'd wanted. Still perspiration ran down my back. They might have been young, but they'd been fast and strong.

"Soldiers advancing quickly. They must have heard the fight." Lars's voice pulled my attention down the road.

I jerked my head toward a pile of bricks.

Dante nodded and joined me.

Boots crunched on loose stone as the soldiers approached. They stopped a few yards away.

I peered through a space in the shattered stone.

"Crynn Dayholt! Soriah wants to speak with you." He held up a radio.

20

I shook my head at Dante. No way would I expose our location. If Sharon wanted to speak with me, she'd contact the radio in our control room.

"We know you're here. The dead monsters give you away," the soldier said. "You can't win this war. Come out and work with us."

Not a chance. I moved backward, being careful with each placement of my foot. When I reached the end, I slipped sideways through a narrow opening and waited for Dante. Once he joined me, we stayed low and raced toward the compound.

"Are they following?" I asked Lars.

"No. They're milling around like idiots. If you'd had a gun you could have picked them off one-by-one."

A gun wouldn't have allowed me to work off some of my fear and frustration like a sword had. "Has Sharon tried contacting me?"

"The radio has flickered a couple of times, but it's facing the wall."

I'd see what she wanted after checking on Fawke.

Dante followed me into the safety of the compound. "Thanks."

"Did me some good, too." He grinned. "Anytime you need a fighting partner look me up. I'm hitting the shower."

I went in the opposite direction to the infirmary.

Rory sat in the chair beside Fawke's bed dabbing his face with a wet rag. "His fever isn't breaking."

"There has to be something we can do." I glanced at Rupert.

"I'm doing all I can. We'll keep fluids down him, sponge baths…and wait."

I didn't want to wait. I wanted him to get out of that bed and help me. Guide me. Make me feel safe. I blinked back tears and brushed the hair away from his face as I leaned close and whispered, "Come back to me. I need you."

Choking back a sob, I whirled and raced for the control room. Anything to keep my thoughts off the possibility of losing Fawke. He'd been the first face I'd laid eyes on after jumping from that helicopter. I needed to see his face every day.

In the control room, I turned the radio monitor around and pressed the call button. When Sharon appeared, I blurted, "What? Did you actually think me stupid enough to reveal my location to a handful of soldiers?"

"I have no idea what you're talking about." A thin smile spread across her face. "I see you weren't the only Stalker to survive. How is Fawke doing?"

"I'll kill you for that." My hands curled into fists.

"That's too bad. He would have made a good soldier."

I almost corrected her assumption that he was dead, but let the matter lie. The more secrets I could keep from her, the better we'd all be.

"I'm a busy woman, Miss Dayholt. If there's no purpose to this call, I will take my leave." The screen flickered off.

I turned the monitor back toward the wall and headed for the jail cell. I couldn't wait for Fawke before questioning who I hoped would be our new recruits. I flagged Ezra down on my way and had him accompany me.

His expression grew grave when I told him of Fawke's condition. "It's better to have more than one person doing the questioning." Next to Fawke, I trusted his judgment the most.

"He'll—"

"Do not tell me he'll be fine! I'm tired of hearing those words. No one knows, do they?" I glared.

He held up his hands. "Fine. Make yourself crazy rushing around."

"I'm staying busy with worthwhile work." I whirled and continued my march to the cell.

Ezra was right. My mood bordered on manic as I tried to find ways to stay busy and not dwell on Fawke lying on his stomach on a hospital bed.

As we walked, I told him of mine and Dante's venture from the compound. "Sharon didn't seem to know about the soldiers we saw."

"Maybe they're more deserters." He shrugged. "We're bound to get some as Soriah sends more and more people out of the white city and into the army camp. What better way to escape than to enlist?"

I glanced up at him. "That's a good point." Could

we create a large enough army from the very ones Soriah sent?

Stan approached the bars as we entered the room. "Ready to let us out?"

"Some questions first." I pulled up a chair, Ezra doing the same.

"Why desert?" I asked.

"Can't stomach the atrocities." He sat in a chair on the other side of the bars. "The camp is overcrowded. We're told to shoot any civilians on sight. If they aren't on Soriah's side, they're considered an enemy."

"We encountered soldiers today using a radio to try and lure me out of hiding." I crossed my arms. "Said Soriah wanted to talk to me."

He nodded. "Deserters. If you would've confronted them, they would have said 'we want to come'. Same as Morrison and I did. It's the code word."

"Maybe you should have told me that sooner. Why didn't they say that upfront?"

He shrugged. "I don't know. Maybe one of them couldn't be trusted. If you'd have stepped out, they most likely would have disposed of that person."

"We want to come?" I frowned.

He chuckled. "Can't really say where, can we? We had no idea this place existed. Thought maybe you were holed up on the mountain. Found remnants of civilization, but it had been empty for weeks."

"That used to be the location of Rebel City." I tilted my head. "This place is much better."

"Where is this place?"

I grinned. "Underground. Now, what do you

have to offer this community if we allow you to join us?"

He gave a grin of his own. "I can get you inside the white city. My father helped build the secret tunnels. There are blueprints in my backpack."

"Your backpack has been searched."

"I wouldn't put them where they could easily be found, now would I?"

"I'll get it." Ezra hurried from the room, returning a few minutes later with the soldier's pack. "Where is it?"

"Feel around the lining. You'll find some raised stitches. The prints are between the lining and the canvas."

Ezra ripped the stitches and pulled out a folded sheet of paper. He held it up for me to see.

Bingo. I stared at an intricate maze of tunnels with an entrance we could access. "Let them out."

"Could be a trap," Ezra said.

"Could be." But then again, Stan could be telling the truth. I was willing to take the risk for the chance to get inside of Soriah. "Let's build our army." I turned back to Stan. "How do we get a hold of the deserters?"

"You can't." He stepped out of the cell Ezra unlocked. "They have to find you."

Which meant more trips away from the compound. More risks at getting caught. "Any way we can get into your armory without risking getting caught?"

"Each group of deserters will bring what weapons they can. It's the safest way."

"Why wasn't Fawke killed?" My throat clogged.

"It's you Soriah wants. It's you the people follow. They needed him to break and tell them how to find you."

"I'm just a girl." Not yet nineteen. Nowhere near a fearsome warrior.

He laughed. "A girl who can lead a rebellion that has a chance of success. You're the face of freedom, Crynn Dayholt."

My mouth fell open. The spinning of a wheel. A needle landing on black. Surviving a city crawling with Malignants. These had made me a hero in these people's eyes. "It could be anyone," I said softly.

"But it's you." Ezra clapped me on the back. "Let's get these guys something to eat."

Fawke woke me three days later by placing his hand on my head. I'd fallen asleep leaning forward on his mattress. "Crynn."

My eyes opened. "You're here."

"I'm here." He gave a weak smile. "How long was I out?"

"Three days." I straightened, rolling the kinks from my shoulders. I told him about going into the city, the soldiers, the blueprints, and how to find more deserters. "I haven't gone out since. I'm waiting on you."

"You shouldn't have waited. Time is of the essence."

"Training has continued." I moved back as Rupert came to check Fawke's bandages.

"Looking good. How do you feel?"

"Better. Weak."

"Want to try sitting up?"

Fawke nodded and the doctor helped him to a

sitting position. "My back's a bit tight."

"It will be. There's a lot of scarring. Try getting up for a few minutes each day, but don't overdo it."

"I'd like my first time up to be the dining room. I hate being fed like a baby."

"Lean on me." I helped him up.

We made our way slowly to the dining hall. Everyone stood and cheered when we entered, clearly happy to see Fawke up and about. I helped him to a chair and motioned for someone to bring him food.

"Welcome back." Ezra straddled a chair at our table. "Gave us quite the scare. Crynn has been a crazy person since you took with the fever. Impossible to live with."

Fawke gave me an amused glance. "How about introducing me to Stan and Morrison?"

I snapped my fingers and waved the two over. "This is Fawke Newton. He helps me lead these people."

The men shook hands and sat at Fawke's invitation. "We can get into Soriah?"

"Yep." Stan grinned.

"One of those tunnels go to the palace?"

"Absolutely."

"Know the location of Cane's apartment?"

"Sure do." Stan's chest puffed out. "All we got to do is get inside, then open the gate to let our fighters swarm the place."

"Glad to see you, son." Anna wrapped her arms around Fawke's neck from behind and kissed the top of his head. "What Stan doesn't know, I do. I can get you where you want to go."

"You'll stay here, mom." He leaned his head back. "I won't risk your life. Your's or Crynn's mother."

Her brow lowered. "I'm still the mother here, and I'll do as I see fit. Everyone is needed to win this fight. I'm sure Carla will agree." She motioned her head toward my mom.

I knew better than to argue when my mom had her mind set. "I don't like it either, Fawke, but I'd rather they were with us than trying to help on their own."

"Listen to her, son. She's smart." Anna tossed me a smile and headed for the kitchen, returning later with a tray of meat and vegetables which she set in the middle of the table. "Eat up, then back to bed."

Fawke sighed, but dug in like a starving man.

Everyone else slipped away, leaving us alone.

Fawke may eat the food as if he hadn't eaten in months, but I drank in every feature of his face as if I'd never see him again. Stubble covered his usually bald head. Weariness creased his forehead and clouded his blue eyes. Still, he sat across from me breathing and alive. For that I gave thanks.

"Crynn to control room," came over the loudspeaker.

I groaned.

"Go on. I'll get someone else to help me back to bed." Fawke reached for a glass of water. "Tomorrow, I'd like to go with you. See what's going on for myself."

I gave him a tender kiss on the cheek and waved Ezra back over. "See he gets back to bed safely, please."

"Will do, boss." He helped Fawke to his feet.

Knowing he'd be alright, I went to see why Lars had summoned me.

"Take a look at this. I think it's the same soldiers from a few days ago." He pointed to the computer monitor.

Five bodies hung from a scaffolding. Their heads had been mounted on a stake at their feet. A very clear warning to anyone wanting to follow their path. Unfortunately, some didn't listen.

In the distance came three more. If we didn't meet these three, they could suffer the same fate as the previous five.

Time to start recruiting.

21

"I'm coming." Fawke stared from the doorway as Dante and I chose our weapons.

"You aren't ready." I turned my attention back to the choices of guns.

"You don't have time to argue with me."

I scowled. He spoke the truth. Three lives depended on us moving quickly. "Fine. You're an adult."

"Thanks for noticing."

"Do you still want me along?" Dante glanced from Fawke to me.

"Yes. Fawke won't be much use if we get into a fight." I slung a gun strap over my shoulder.

"A tight back won't stop me." Fawke crossed his arms and grimaced.

"Right." I arched a brow. "You're in great shape." Brushing past him, I led Dante to the side door and waited for Fawke.

He showed up loaded down with a backpack and rocket launcher as if he had something to prove. Why wouldn't he allow others to care for him? He'd taken care of so many.

I shook my head and opened the door, stepping out first. "Be my eyes, Lars."

"Head west. They're keeping to the shadows and coming this way. I think the army might have a small inkling of where we're located."

General proximity, maybe. I took a fresh look around the theme park. Looked like nothing more than a pile of cement and bricks. I stepped over and around obstacles as I headed in the direction Lars told me to go. The crunching behind let me know the other two followed.

I spotted a lone Malignant to my right. With Fawke in the condition he was, I let it go. Where there was one, there were more. Why were the creatures returning to the burned-out city?

"See that half of a building in front of you? Take a right," Lars said. "The Malignant is headed for the soldiers. You'll most likely hear the fight before you see it."

Hopefully, the men would be smart enough not to fire a gun and alert the army. Since it was past dawn, they'd be sure to send out a party to dispose of the deserters.

The Malignant screamed. I rounded the corner of a toppled wall in time to see it leap on the back of a soldier. Rushing forward, I plunged my sword into the back of its head.

"Thank you." The soldier bent at the knees and vomited. After swiping his mouth with the back of his hand, he said, "We want to come."

I glanced in the direction of the army camp, then at my comrades before giving the okay. "We have to blindfold you."

They stood without argument. Although Stanley had told me more would come, and these three had spoken the passwords, I still wouldn't allow them to see how to reach the compound until they'd been there a few days and proven their trustworthiness. I would not compromise on that.

After a quick check of their packs, finding food, ammo, and medical supplies, not counting the weapons they carried, I looped them all together with a length of rope. "Be careful where you plant your feet. You don't need to fall. We'll move as quickly as you can manage."

"Good, because they'll be coming for us."

"Army patrol on its way," Lars said. "They're bulldozing debris out of their way as they come."

Which would slow them down this time, but make traveling easier in the future. For them and for us. I tied the rope to Dante's belt and motioned for Fawke to take the lead.

"Uh, we have a problem," Lars said.

"What?"

"Helicopter in the air and headed right for you. There's a parking garage, or what's left of one, half a block to your left. Hurry."

In the distance, came the thwump-thwump of helicopter blades. I yanked the blindfolds off the faces of the soldiers and cut the rope. "Run."

No one needed to be told twice. We hurtled over piles of rubbish in our haste. One soldier fell, his leg trapped between two cement blocks.

Fawke stopped, his eyes narrowed. "Aren't you the man who laid the whip to my back? Laughed and said what a pleasure you'd get from the act?"

"No." He paled.

"He is," another soldier with a soft voice said. "He said if we didn't take him with us, he'd cry out an alarm. We planned on telling you before we reached your hiding place."

"Keep screaming," Fawke said. "The Malignants will find you."

"We don't have time for this." I thrust my sword into the man's heart. I'd said I would kill the man who'd whipped Fawke. Now to face the man who had given the order. The sergeant. I wiped the blade of my sword on the dead man's uniform shirt, grabbed his pack, and then resumed my sprint toward the parking garage, Fawke on my heels having relieved the soldier of his gun.

Why would the soldiers wait until we were closer to home before alerting us the other man's deceit? Something didn't make sense. Instinct told me none of them could be trusted.

Inside the garage, I held my sword at the throat of one while Fawke followed suit with the other. "You should have said something right away." I pressed the tip to the man's skin. "Who are you?"

"So, he could shoot off that pistol he carried and give us away? No thanks." His eyes widened. "I gave you the password, he didn't. That's because he didn't know it. Mole here is good. You can trust us. I'm Norb."

Mole turned out to be a woman. She'd removed her cap and shaken out shoulder length blond hair. "I guess time will tell whether you can trust us, Crynn Dayholt. Don't look so surprised. Everyone knows your name, thanks to Sharon. The army is given a briefing every evening right after mess. I'm hoping my brother Stanley is already a part of your group?"

I nodded, then lowered my sword, turning my attention to the outside where a helicopter passed low overhead. Gunfire erupted from the machine under one wing, cutting the shrieks of Malignants off mid-cry.

"Oh, and you might want to know that Soriah is sending more Malignants to slow you down." Mole smirked. "They're turning those in the prisons into those things."

My blood ran cold. "What?"

"Soriah dropped the original bombs, right? The ones that destroyed our world and created those mutants? Well, they're doing it again. Just a few at a time to keep you occupied with the monsters rather than the army."

"How do you know this?" Fawke asked, leaning against a wall.

"I overheard the commander and the sergeant talking on my way to the latrine. They didn't know anyone was inside and stopped right outside my door. That's helpful, right? My brother said it would help you make up your mind about taking us with you if we had something to contribute."

Their ability and willingness to fight was enough for me, but this news was huge. Eb had told us why Soriah dropped the bombs in the first place, but to use humans to make monsters seemed far-fetched even for President Cane. Another means of population control in addition to causing me trouble? I needed to contact Sharon and see whether I could get any information out of her.

The helicopter circled around again. I could make out the sounds of rubble being shoved in front of a bulldozer growing closer. We needed to move.

"Lars. Where can we go? We're sitting ducks here."

"I don't know. You'll be spotted if you step out. Can you move deeper into the garage?"

I glanced at Fawke.

"I'll scout it out." He dashed away.

"Do you believe her story about the Malignants and Soriah?" Dante asked, moving closer to me and lowering his voice.

"I don't know. Seems unreal. We can ask Stanley about whether or not he has a sister."

"He doesn't," Lars said. "I asked as soon as she said it."

I glanced back to Mole and grinned. The nickname now made sense. Either I'd killed an innocent man or Norb was the only soldier telling the truth.

I spotted the radio she pulled from her pack at the same time Fawke returned. Before she could give away our location, Fawke had slit her throat.

"Thanks for the tip, Norb," I said. "Did the man I kill whip Fawke?"

"Yes, but they threatened his family if he didn't. Said he had to make it good or his son would receive every lash that failed to rip Fawke's skin." He stared at the body of Mole. "That's the commander's woman. He won't like that you've killed her."

"Everything she said about the Malignants was a lie?" I asked.

"Probably," Fawke answered for him. "We can move deeper into the garage, but there are a lot of nests in there. Lots of babies waiting for their mothers to return. We couldn't have picked a less safe place to hole up in."

With only four of us, we'd be no match for Malignant mothers protecting their young. That explained the sightings we'd seen. Not all of the monsters had fled the city. Not until their young could go with them.

"Do we stay and hope the helicopter flies off before the beasts return or do we take our chances outside?" I glanced at the others. This decision posed too much danger either way for me to make it alone.

"I say we leave, staying to the shadows, ducking in and out where we can." Fawke slid his knife back into his belt. "I counted ten nests in there with one to two infants in each one. Like you said earlier, I'll be no good in a fight."

I grabbed one of the dead soldier's packs and tossed the other to Dante. "Let's go."

Outside, Lars directed us to heading west for the time being. "The bulldozer has gotten stuck, but they'll be moving again soon. Worry about the helicopter. If you can see it, the pilot can see you."

"Thank you Captain Obvious," Dante said, stepping from the garage and taking the lead.

I didn't bother blindfolding Norb. We couldn't move fast with him blind. Either he could be trusted or he couldn't. He had known the password. If Stanley didn't vouch for him, we'd get rid of him then.

Whenever we heard the helicopter overhead, we

ducked into the nearest alcove or building or ducked behind rubble. Anything to give us shelter. The rumble of an engine alerted me to the fact the bulldozer moved again.

"Here." Dante pointed to a hole under a collapsed building. "If we push the packs ahead of us, we might be able to crawl through here. It'll bring us out close to the park."

"Chance it." I'd rather die buried under rubble than beheaded or shot to pieces by the army. Being the smallest of the four, crawling would be a cinch.

Dante's large frame dislodged dust and flakes of cement as he belly-crawled forward. Norb followed, then Fawke, with me taking up the rear.

I sneezed at the dust cloud created by the sliding of our packs. My sword banged against my thigh.

Fawke let out the occasional groan whenever what was over us scraped against his back. Already tiny bits of red bled through the camouflage shirt he wore.

"You okay?" I asked.

"Yeah." He continued moving forward. "Nothing a pain pill won't fix."

And a good scrubbing. I blinked against the grit in my eyes.

"Hold up." Dante stopped fast enough my head banged into Fawke's rear end. "Need to check things out before we crawl into the open."

The light in our crawl space improved when he moved. Seconds later, his face appeared in the opening. "All clear."

"All clear," Lars said, "but that dozer is getting closer and headed this way. You need to get inside before they start on this lot."

    If they cleared the lot, they'd expose our doors.

22

I led the way in a mad dash across the theme park lot and into the underground compound. Inside, I turned to the others. "We have to cut them off. Gather our fighters in the training room."

"First battle. Awesome." Dante raced down the hall.

"Are you sure?" Fawke's brow creased. "Are they ready?"

"They have to be." I hurried to the armory, talking over my shoulder as he followed. "That bulldozer will expose us. We have to stop them before they get here. Lars, how many soldiers?"

"Ten, plus the driver."

Good. We wouldn't need everyone. "We won't have to alert Soriah to our numbers. We'll take our strongest and stop those outside before they reach us." We had to keep this place secret for as long as possible.

In the armory, I set Ezra to work choosing weapons for ten fighters. Fawke went with me to pick those who would follow us into battle.

He naturally gravitated to our core group. "Ezra, Moses, Dante, Gage, Jolt, Kira, Ted and Ned." They each stepped forward as their name was called.

"Not Kira," I said. "She's needed in the infirmary."

She shook her head. "Rupert and Rory can handle things. You need me."

"I'll need you more if I'm injured. Step out of line. No, Roland. You aren't ready."

The boy scowled and stepped back.

"I'll go." Samson, one of the first criminals sent to us, stepped into line.

Fawke nodded. "Thank you. Head to the armory and get suited up."

"I don't want you on the front line." I stopped him in the hall. "Your reflexes will be slow."

"Should I stay in the schoolroom with the children?" His eyes flashed.

"Don't be ridiculous. I need you telling the others what to do. Just no hand-to-hand combat." I crossed my arms and glared. "We can stand here all day and argue or go stop that bulldozer. Which is it?"

"You're infuriating."

"You're stubborn." I tilted my head, a smile tugging at my lips.

He chuckled. "Fine. Have it your way. I'll be the cowardly sergeant leading from behind."

Grinning, I continued to the armory. We didn't have enough riot suits for everyone, but were able to suit up half of us. Those men would be our first offense.

The twins, Ted and Ned, would man the rocket launchers.

Fawke shouted orders as if he'd been fighting his entire life.

I stood to the side watching, knowing I'd be right behind those in the suits. I had a shield, a gun, and my sword. It would be enough.

"We're going head-to-head with them?" Gage paled. "They most likely have a machine gun."

"We'll surround them," Fawke said. "We know this area, they don't. Those with riot gear will approach from the front. The rest will circle around and attack from the rear."

"Do we kill them all?" Dante fastened a belt of ammo over his shoulder.

"Not if they know the password," I said. "Only if they aim to shoot." I shot Fawke a look.

He nodded. "We need everyone we can get. This is the first battle of many. Someday, we'll storm the walls of Soriah. Before that happens, we have an army to cut down to size. We need manpower to accomplish that task."

Armed for war, we left the safety of the compound. Those in suits moved forward, using debris as cover. The rest of us sprinted along the edge of the dried-up field to circle around.

"When we're within hearing distance," Fawke said. "I want you to stand where they can see you and call out. They won't shoot you. You're worth too much alive. But, you will be the perfect distraction to allow the others to get close."

My throat dried up. I nodded. President Cane would want me alive if at all possible.

We left the safety of the tall grass, and I climbed on top of rubble as gunfire erupted. One of the twins fell before Dante raised the rocket launcher.

I waved my arms to alert him to my presence.

He lowered the weapon.

The soldiers turned, guns aimed in my direction.

"I'm Crynn Dayholt. I think you're looking for me." My voice rang across the pitted parking lot that had once held happy park goers. "You're outnumbered. Lower your weapons."

One soldier, foolish enough to think he could take me down, raised his gun. Ezra shot him, dropping him like a rock.

"Anyone else feeling lucky?" I held my arms out to my side. "Who is in charge here?"

"I am. You're under arrest, Miss Dayholt, for conspiring against Soriah." A man with three stripes on his sleeve stepped forward.

"Do you plan on taking us all in?" I motioned for the others to join me, while those in riot gear moved forward opposite us.

The sergeant slowly turned in a circle before facing me again. "I'd say we're pretty evenly matched."

"I'd say you were wrong."

Dante raised the launcher again.

"You'll be blown to bits before you can fire that gun on your hip. Surrender."

"More will come, Miss Dayholt. Hundreds. You can't survive this."

"I'm thinking only of today." I raised my gun and fired, the shot taking him in the knee. "Should I try for your other leg?"

He lay on the ground howling as the other soldiers lay their weapons on the ground and put their hands over their heads. Two, keeping their eyes on me, pulled the wounded sergeant to the side of the bulldozer.

"Separate." I stepped from the pile and marched toward the soldiers. We'd have to kill any that didn't know the password.

Fawke stood over the sergeant, pressing his booted foot against the shattered knee. "I ought to hang you from a pole and give you one more lash than you ordered I be given."

"Then why don't you?"

A sneer curled Fawke's lips. "Oh, you'll hang as an example, but I don't have the time for forty-two lashes." He turned back to our group. "Tie everyone's hands behind their back."

When that was done, Fawke and I questioned each soldier in turn, making sure the others were far enough away not to hear their answers. "Got anything to say?"

"Go to hell."

My heart dropped more with each soldier we disposed of. I didn't like the new Crynn, the one who could kill with such ease. Curse the wheel that sent me here. Curse the leader who died, making me have to take his place. Only the hope of a better future for mankind kept me going.

I glanced to where Ted cradled his dying brother's head in his lap. We'd lose more of our original group before this was over.

"We want to come," a soldier whispered.

"Who's we?" I arched a brow. "You stand alone."

"The word is we, not I." Sweat poured down his

brow. "A man or woman on their own will not survive what is coming."

"Are there more of them here today?"

He shook his head. "No, but there is a convoy coming. They are all wanting to come."

"How do you know this?" Hope leaped within me.

"A secure channel on the radio on my belt."

I grinned at Fawke. Our army was coming. "Prove we can trust you by hanging the sergeant from that light post."

The man scampered to do as ordered. With Ezra's help, the sergeant was hoisted up, his legs flailing, until he hung limp. Only one other soldier, a woman, knew the password. I ordered her to gather all weapons and supplies from her dead comrades.

As we all headed back to the compound, I had Dante put the bulldozer out of commission. He yanked a few wires from the engine and slid them into his pack. "In case we need this thing someday." He flashed a grin and led the group home.

Once the others were inside, Ted carrying Ned, Fawke and I paused outside. "It was too easy," he said.

"Yes." I glanced to where I could barely make out the white of Soriah's walls. "They wanted us to approach their soldiers. What they don't know is that every time we do, they lose one or two. Our numbers grow while theirs get smaller. Eventually, they'll run out of soldiers to send."

"All we have to do is stay strong until we outnumber them."

"Exactly." I leaned into him. "We can win this

fight, Fawke."

"Yes, but we will lose friends."

That's the part I hated. People I loved would die. I had to keep my mind on the bigger picture of freedom without Cane and his white city.

"Look out, Soriah," I whispered, "the fight is coming."

Like an omen, a flock of black birds flew toward the white walls of Soriah.

Don't miss the next book, The Fight,

Website at www.cynthiahickey.com

Multi-published and Amazon and ECPA Best-Selling author Cynthia Hickey, writing as Cynthia Melton, has sold close to a million copies of her works since 2013. She has taught a Continuing Education class at the 2015 American Christian Fiction Writers conference, several small ACFW chapters and RWA chapters, and small writer retreats. She and her husband run the small press, Winged Publications, which includes some of the CBA's best well-known authors. She lives in Arizona and Arkansas, becoming a snowbird, with her husband and one dog. She has ten grandchildren who keep her busy and tell everyone they know that "Nana is a writer".